# GUARDIAN SPIRITS

# OTHER BOOKS FROM JORDAN L. HAWK:

*Hainted*

<u>Whyborne & Griffin:</u>
*Widdershins*
*Threshold*
*Stormhaven*
*Necropolis*
*Bloodline*
*Hoarfrost*
*Maelstrom*
*Fallow*
*Draakenwood*

<u>SPECTR:</u>
*Hunter of Demons*
*Master of Ghouls*
*Reaper of Souls*
*Eater of Lives*
*Destroyer of Worlds*
*Summoner of Storms*
*Mocker of Ravens*
*Drinker of Blood*
*Breaker of Chains*

<u>Hexworld:</u>
*Hexbreaker*
*Hexmaker*
*Hexslayer*

# GUARDIAN SPIRITS

*Spirits Book 3*

## JORDAN L. HAWK

H

Guardian Spirits © 2018 Jordan L. Hawk
ISBN: 978-1717339973

Cover art © 2018 Jordan L. Hawk

Edited by Annetta Ribken

*For Beth.*

# CHAPTER 1

**THE DEAD MAN** refused to answer.

Vincent rose out of a trance with no foreign taste on his tongue. Only the lingering traces of the cinnamon cachous he used to cleanse his palate of more ghostly flavors. The air against his skin was merely cool, a crisp fall evening, rather than the icy cold indicative of a spirit drawing energy from the atmosphere. Hands gripped his from either side, both firm; if they had succeeded, he would have expected Lizzie's to tremble.

"I failed," he said, and opened his eyes.

He sat at the séance table in the upstairs parlor of their little shop. The curtains had been drawn against the gaslights illuminating the Baltimore street outside, leaving them in near-total darkness. Even so, he felt the presence of the living in the room with him. Elizabeth Devereaux, his fellow medium, held his right hand. Jocelyn Strauss, seventeen years old and a genius when it came to machines and mathematics, sat directly across from him. And Henry Strauss, inventor —and Vincent's lover—gripped Vincent's left hand tightly.

"You didn't fail," Henry said. "He simply chose not to answer."

"We could try again," Lizzie suggested, though she didn't sound at all pleased at the prospect.

"No." A weariness more spiritual than physical weighed on Vincent's bones. "He isn't going to answer us. Neither of them are."

"Cowards," Henry said staunchly. "Jo, could you open the curtains?"

The circle broke apart, and Jo tugged back the curtains while Henry lit the lamps. Warm gaslight soon filled every corner of the slightly shabby room, gleaming off the apparatus Henry insisted on setting up at every séance: Franklin Bells, which would ring when the presence of a spirit charged the air, thermometer, barometer, and even a copper grounding rod should the summoned spirit turn violent. Not to suggest they had expected the spirit they sought tonight to be dangerous, but Henry always insisted on being prepared.

Since Vincent had spent most of his life drifting along with the currents, Henry's tendency to plan ahead came as an unexpected comfort.

Jo glanced from Vincent to Lizzie, her brown face drawn with worry. "I'm sorry you couldn't contact your mentor."

"The spirits are under no obligation to answer us," Lizzie said. She ran a tired hand over her jaw, frowned slightly as her fingers encountered a trace of stubble. Her shaving and plucking regimen was immaculate, even when it was only the four of them, and her gesture now told Vincent how heavily the situation weighed on her.

"I'd say Dunne damned well owes you an explanation." Henry folded his arms over his chest. "Pardon my language, ladies," he added when Lizzie cast him a stern look, "but it's true."

James Dunne hadn't just been Lizzie and Vincent's mentor—he'd plucked them from the streets as children and given them the first home in which they'd ever been welcome. Taught them not only how to be mediums, but how to be decent people. By the end of their apprenticeship, he and Lizzie would have done anything for him. Or for Sylvester Ortensi, who had been like a kindly uncle to them.

Bad enough a malevolent spirit had possessed Vincent and used his hands to kill Dunne. But then Ortensi revealed to them that he and Dunne had hidden things from them. They had been searching for something, and were desperate enough to turn to necromancy to find it.

Desperate enough to murder anyone in their way.

Ortensi died before he could give them any answers. Hence the séance to contact the one person who might: Dunne himself.

Henry held out the silver amulet Vincent had entrusted him with at the start of the séance. The amulet guarded against involuntary possession; after his encounter with the dark spirit which had killed Dunne, Vincent seldom went without it. Unfortunately, channeling spirits required temporarily lending them his voice and body, which meant he had to take the amulet off for séances. "Thank you," Vincent said, and fastened it around his neck again.

"Is there anything else we can do?" Jo asked. She perched on one of the chairs, her lower lip caught between her teeth as she pondered. "Perhaps if we used the Wimshurst Machine? Added more energy to the air?"

"I don't think it's lack of energy that's the problem," Lizzie said with a heavy sigh. "Dunne has surely passed on. If he lingered on this side of the veil, perhaps...but he didn't. And we can't compel him to come back and give us answers, no matter how badly we might want to."

"As I said before, the man is a coward." Henry gave a little sniff, even as he began to clear away his instrumentation from the table. "If he withheld things from you, he should put forth a little effort. Set the record straight, rather than leaving you with such uncertainty."

"Dunne wasn't a coward," Vincent said, almost reflexively. Even knowing what he did, even suspecting what he did, the instinct to defend his mentor still remained.

Lizzie pressed a hand to her forehead. "I don't know what to think. We've tried spirit writing, psychometry, and now channeling, all to no avail."

"We have to keep looking." Vincent rose and went to the writing desk against the wall. Pulling open a drawer, he removed the journal they'd found among Ortensi's things at the hotel in Devil's Walk, after he'd died. Unfortunately, it had been a relatively new journal, started just before he'd departed Europe for the final time. If they'd had more money in the bank, perhaps they could have traveled to France, where he'd spent the last several years. Maybe his earlier journals were still there and would have yielded answers.

Most of the journal offered nothing beyond the ordinary details of a medium's life. It confirmed what Ortensi had already told them. The murderous spirit of Devil's Walk had been summoned by a necromantic talisman. Rather than destroy such an abomination, Ortensi had hoped to take it for himself. The only real clues lay in his final entry, made the day they'd arrived to assist him.

*It's so good to see Lizzie and Vincent again. I still can't believe James is gone. He understood the operation of the Grand Harmonium far better than I. Vincent's account of the spirit that killed James troubles me. It wasn't like James to be taken so unaware. Some spirits conceal their true nature, but those usually have a motive of some sort, even if only to spread chaos and fear. This one slew James and simply...left.*

*As for James...I try not to mourn him. The impulse is foolish—death is but sleep, and as easy to wake from. I just need a little more time, and I'm sure I'll be able to recreate the Astral Key. Then the Grand Harmonium will be restored, and James returned to my side. But it is hard not to miss him.*

*What might our lives have been, if Arabella hadn't betrayed us? Damn her! We would have made the world a paradise, instead of the mire it is.*

*No matter. My youth might be gone, but once the Harmonium is restored, surely such things will be of no consequence. James might be temporarily beyond my reach, but at least I still have Vincent and Lizzie. They're strong. They passed every test.*

*They won't fail the way Arabella failed.*

*I must separate Vincent from Mr. Strauss. Strauss represents the worst impulses, is possessed of the lowest of natures. He is filled with ambition and greed. If Strauss learned of the Grand Harmonium, he'd wish to take it apart and sell off the pieces for profit. He sees only the parts of a thing, not the wonder of the whole. Vincent's tendency toward loyalty may prove inconvenient in this instance. I'll observe them both closely tomorrow, and think on how best to drive a wedge in between.*

The entry ended there. Vincent shut the journal with a snap. "What the blazes is the Grand Harmonium?" he asked aloud, just as he had again and again since first reading the words on the train back from Devil's Walk. "What is the Astral Key he meant to recreate? And who is —or was—Arabella?"

"As for the Grand Harmonium, presumably Ortensi didn't travel the world in search of the means to perfect a musical instrument." Henry took off his spectacles and began to clean them with a handkerchief. "I still maintain it sounds like some sort of machine."

"Ortensi didn't seem very pleased with our machines," Jo pointed out. "Or you, Henry."

"I'm heartbroken to have garnered his disapproval," Henry said dryly.

"He said it would return Dunne to his side." The corners of Lizzie's mouth turned down into a tight frown. "That sounds like necromancy."

Vincent shook his head. Necromancy—the forced summoning of the unwilling dead—might be wrong, but that hadn't stopped people from studying it thoroughly. "'Death is but sleep, and as easy to wake from.'" He'd stared at the journal entry so often he had memorized the phrase. "That doesn't sound like any necromancy I've ever heard of."

"Besides," Jo added, "If he meant to simply compel Dunne's ghost, he could have just used the necromantic talisman he took from Mr. Fitzwilliam in Devil's Walk."

"Precisely." Vincent ran a hand through his hair in frustration.

"Some other means of contacting the dead, perhaps? A more reliable means than a séance, but without the compulsion of necromancy?"

"We could speculate endlessly," Henry said. "At least it doesn't sound like the Grand Harmonium is in a state to be used. Not without this Astral Key, whatever it might be."

"There must be answers, somewhere," Lizzie said. "If only Dunne had kept a journal. If we still had his house, or the shop in New York…"

"Well, we don't," Vincent said. "And honestly, I doubt it would help even if we did. We lived and worked with him for years and never suspected him of keeping secrets. He wouldn't have left anything where we had a hope of finding it."

"There must be something." Lizzie stared out the window, as though the answers might appear on the glass. "We just have to keep searching."

Henry frowned at her words. But he only said, "It's late. We should get some sleep. Take my bed, Lizzie, so you don't have to walk back to your apartment."

"The sheets might be a little dusty," Jo added with a sly grin.

Henry shot her a quelling look. Not that she was wrong. Ever since Vincent had moved into the little room above the workshop out back, he and Henry had shared its bed every night. Henry kept a few things in what had previously been his bedroom, for the sake of space, but for all practicalities he and Vincent lived together.

Which wasn't something Vincent had ever envisioned for himself. But then, he'd never envisioned meeting someone like Henry, either.

Lizzie hesitated visibly, her gaze going again to the darkness outside the window. It was too late to find a cab, even if they'd had the money to spare, which meant either Vincent or Henry would have to walk her home. "Very well," she said at last. "I'll leave at first light, then return for Mrs. Burwell's spirit writing session tomorrow afternoon. Hopefully her departed mother will be more amenable to contact than Dunne."

Henry followed Vincent across the darkened yard to the workshop. He'd originally used the small building to conduct experiments which needed more space than was available in the store's back room, or which produced smells that might drive away customers. And he still did; the downstairs was a single open space packed with tables and equipment. He and Vincent had converted the upper floor, however, into a cozy apartment.

They ascended the outside staircase to the apartment's door. Once inside, Vincent didn't bother to light the sitting room's lamp, instead walking straight through to the darkened bedroom. Henry winced—this wasn't like him. Ordinarily, Vincent would stay up to absurd hours, reading poetry or novels while he lounged on the couch in his oriental robe. Then he'd sleep until noon, before spending another hour choosing his clothing and pomading his hair. For him to retire to bed at such a relatively early time didn't bode well.

While Henry lit the night candle, Vincent began to disrobe, his movements quick and efficient. A flash of anger coursed through Henry, directed not at Vincent, but at the accursed Dunne.

When he'd first met Vincent and Lizzie, they'd been desperately trying to save the occult shop that had belonged to their dead mentor. They always spoke of the man in tones not just of affection, but awe. As though he were somehow more—better—than human. Flawless as an angel.

No doubt all of his treatment of them hadn't been a self-serving lie. But their stint in Devil's Walk made it clear the man had concealed a great deal. Lied to them about fundamental things.

No wonder they'd both been adrift ever since. Desperate to reconcile the things Ortensi had told them, with the idealized memory of their mentor. They were haunted…though not literally, in this case.

Henry would have some strong words for Dunne, should they ever manage to contact the scoundrel. How dare he put Vincent and Lizzie through such pain? If he had truly cared for them, he should have included them in whatever grand scheme he and Ortensi had worked toward.

But anger wouldn't help Vincent. Henry pushed it down and stepped behind Vincent, putting his hands lightly at Vincent's waist. "I'm sorry," he said. "What can I do?"

For a moment, Vincent held himself stiffly. Then he sagged back, letting Henry take some of his weight. He was the taller of the two, so Henry pressed his cheek into Vincent's shoulder. The citrus and musk scent of Vincent's cologne filled his nose, and the warmth and heft of his body quickened Henry's blood.

"If I knew, I'd tell you," Vincent said. "You must think us fools, to let ourselves be so obsessed by this."

"Not at all." Henry slid his arms around Vincent's slender waist, pulling him closer. "He was like a father to you. I know how badly losing him hurt." Henry's own father had died when he was but a youth, and God knew he still missed the man. At least his memories hadn't been tainted by post-mortem revelations. "I can only imagine how you must feel now. Afraid you're being disrespectful of his memory by doubting him, but worried your doubt is justified."

"Exactly." Vincent turned to face him, then bent for a kiss. "I'm sick of thinking about it."

"Shall I give you something else to think about for a while?"

"Yes," Vincent said fervently, and wound his arms around Henry's shoulders, hauling him close.

Their kiss began leisurely, before deepening. Vincent's warm mouth tasted of cinnamon. He'd already removed coat, tie, and vest, so Henry set about unbuttoning his shirt an inch at a time, slowly exposing the sienna skin beneath. Henry paused to make sure he paid Vincent's dark brown nipples proper attention with his lips and teeth, and was rewarded with a soft groan.

Henry shoved down Vincent's bracers, then peeled off his shirt, pausing just long enough to carefully hang it up. He'd learned early on that Vincent's clothing was an armor of sorts. Whites expected an Indian to look a certain way; when confronted with the impeccably dressed Vincent, they tended to offer more respect than they would have otherwise. It was a bit of stupid thinking Henry had fallen into himself, when they'd first met.

Henry made sure to brush his hand against Vincent's erection more than strictly necessary as he unbuttoned Vincent's trousers. Drawers came next, and Henry sank to his knees to take Vincent's cock in his mouth. His taste, the heavy feel of him against Henry's tongue, sent a rush of blood to Henry's own prick, and he moaned as he took his lover to the root.

Vincent's hands tangled in Henry's hair, tightened—then pushed at him. "Not like this. I want you to come in my mouth at the same time."

Henry slid off reluctantly, giving a last lap at the slit as he did so. "Get on the bed."

Henry undressed quickly, but when he turned back to the bed, he stopped just to admire the sight. Vincent sprawled against the pale sheets, his cock dark with desire, his black eyes shining with lust. God, he was beautiful, all long legs and shapely muscles. He wore his thick black hair cut long, in imitation of the style Oscar Wilde had set on his American tour, and it spread across the pillow in a halo.

Henry in no way deserved him, but was grateful every day to have him anyway.

"I love you," Henry said.

Vincent's expression softened. "I love you, too. Now come here and let me show you how much."

The sensation of Vincent's bare skin against his never ceased to send a thrill through Henry. For so long, his only encounters had been of the sort done in back alleys, quick and furtive, removing only as much clothing as necessary. The luxury of having a lover and a bed still felt new and exciting. Vincent's arms snaked around Henry's chest, pulling him tight, their thighs and cocks pressed together. Henry kissed Vincent thoroughly, moving his hips in a slow grind, sending slow shocks of pleasure through them both.

Vincent drew back just a bit. "I want you in my mouth."

"Mmm." Henry grinned and nuzzled what he knew to be a sensitive spot on Vincent's neck, drawing a gasp from him. "I'm not going to refuse such an offer."

He reversed his position on the bed, and they lay on their sides. Henry kissed Vincent's strong thighs, then caught his cock between his lips once again. The slow, teasing lick of Vincent's tongue along his own prick made Henry whimper.

"Impatient," Vincent said, his lips moving against the very tip of Henry's erection. Then he slid down, engulfing him in wet heat.

They clung to each other, hands roaming across whatever skin they could reach, mouths fastened on one another. Vincent's tongue was clever with more than words, and soon Henry found himself fighting to hold back. He tried focusing on the prick filling his own mouth, but Vincent's taste and feel, his little moans, only added to Henry's arousal. He let out a muffled sound of warning, balls tightening, and Vincent groaned around him as he came.

He tried to keep sucking as he spent, rhythm lost, until Vincent's thighs trembled and bitterness flooded Henry's throat in return.

They lay silent for a moment, breath coming in short gasps. Despite the cool night, a light film of sweat slicked their skin. Henry pressed his lips to Vincent's thigh.

"Come here, Henry," Vincent murmured sleepily.

Henry didn't want to move, but he clambered around until he was facing the right way in the bed again. Vincent had rolled onto his back, eyelids already drooping shut. The tension had eased from his handsome features, at least for the moment, and a rush of emotion shook Henry, so strong it threatened to cut off his breath.

"I'd do anything for you," he whispered.

Vincent's generous mouth turned up into a smile. "Then salt the door."

"You just don't want to get up," Henry teased. But he rolled out of bed and did as asked.

Vincent hadn't always slept with a line of salt across the windows and door. But after the malevolent spirit had possessed him and killed Dunne, Vincent feared it was still out there, somewhere. That it might return, despite the passage of time and distance.

Perhaps it wasn't the most logical of fears, but if pouring salt across the doors and windows each night made Vincent feel safer, that was what Henry would do.

Once finished, Henry blew out the candle, then pillowed his head on Vincent's chest. Within moments, Vincent had slipped away into sleep. Henry listened to the beat of his lover's heart beneath his ear. The edge of the silver amulet pressed against his forehead, a silent reminder, along with the salt, of the lingering damage the spirit had done to Vincent's soul.

Had Dunne known there was something unusual about the poltergeist he'd taken Vincent to confront? Vincent insisted there had been no warning, but Henry was less certain of Dunne's honesty in the matter.

The man's other apprentices had died somehow, after all. The ones Dunne had never seen fit to mention to Vincent and Lizzie. They would never have known, if Ortensi hadn't told them.

They weren't the first. They were just the ones who had survived.

Assuming Ortensi hadn't lied to further his own ends. At least they could take the writing in the journal, intended for no one else's eyes, as honest.

Perhaps it was just as well they'd failed to raise Dunne's spirit tonight. The idea of never learning the truth irked Henry…but maybe it was time to put all of this behind them. To let go of the fear and guilt and doubt chaining them to the past. To focus instead on the future of their business, of their family.

Vincent and Lizzie needed something to distract them. The only clientele they'd had as of late had been the ordinary sort: weekly séances, some spirit writing, a few people who wanted them to come investigate odd sounds or cold spots in their houses, none of which had turned out to be due to ghosts. There had been nothing to demand their attention for more than an hour or two at a stretch, leaving them with far too much time to brood.

Well, then. Henry would simply have to find something for them.

What, he didn't know, but if he put his mind to it, surely he could come up with some project to allow them to focus their minds and energy, and let go of Dunne once and for all.

# CHAPTER 2

**THE NEXT MORNING,** Henry began to comb through the various occult journals over breakfast with Jo. Lizzie had already left for her apartment, and Vincent still snored in bed, which left Henry with plenty of time to think.

Mornings had become a favorite ritual. Just Jo and him, spending time together. Normally they ate breakfast, then went to the back room to repair their equipment, or work on building more.

Henry had never expected to find himself in the position of raising a girl. But the rest of the family looked down on Jo due to her black mother, and had either refused to take her in or mistreated her when her parents died. As a result, Henry had found himself the sole guardian of his cousin.

That had been three years ago. She was almost a woman now… which meant he spent a great deal of time worrying about her. They'd had a few vague discussions as to what she might do next. She might go to a college for negro girls, but most of them prepared women to be teachers rather than scientists. Considering Jo was even now doing advanced mathematics for fun over breakfast, he feared she would find such a program of study to be unsatisfying at the least.

"Stop looking at me like that, Henry," she said without glancing up from her calculations.

"You don't know how I was looking at you," he objected.

"You were fretting. Again." She finished her math problem and raised her head. "Go back to worrying about Vincent and Lizzie."

"I'm not worrying about them, either." Henry turned the page of the journal put out by the Baltimore Psychical Society. They'd denied him membership—not that he wanted it, at least not after learning what a bunch of bigoted pricks they were. But their publications were useful when it came to keeping abreast of occult happenings in Maryland and the surrounding states. "I don't worry about anything. I'm carefree as a… a thing that's carefree."

"You're the worst liar I've ever met," Jo replied. "I thought I'd work on the second arc light headlamp this morning. I do wish the batteries weren't so heavy." A faraway look came into her eyes. "Hmm. Perhaps different materials would result in a decrease in size."

"Finish the headlamp before experimenting with the batteries. As for me, I'm going to catch up on my reading." He waved the journal vaguely as proof.

After cleaning up from breakfast, they retired to the store downstairs. Jo disappeared into the workroom in the back, and Henry perched behind the counter.

Within an hour, he was beginning to think the thick journal would yield little in the way of results. He'd hoped to find some inspiration to offer Vincent and Lizzie, a different focus for their thoughts, but nothing presented itself. Some of the articles were at least worth reading, but the editor seemed a bit too uncritical when it came to subjects of a scientific nature.

"This idiot doesn't even understand how magnetism works," he muttered aloud, after one particularly vexing entry.

"Neither do I," Vincent said from behind him. A moment later, his hands settled on Henry's shoulders, and he leaned in to kiss Henry's cheek.

"Yes, but you aren't submitting articles about your theories of 'interplanetary magnetism' to the psychical journals, either," Henry said.

"True." Vincent stepped past him and began to set the storefront to rights. Early sales of the Electro-Séance had been disappointing, despite the prominent display in the window. The public seemed more interested in planchette boards, tarot cards, and oils which did nothing beyond smelling pleasant.

Henry almost skipped over the letters to the editor. The journal had failed to offer any inspiration, and usually the letters were good only for a chuckle or an eye-roll.

One of the longer entries caught his eye, however. He read it, then read it again, excitement growing in his breast.

"Listen to this," he said.

The door opened, and Lizzie let herself in. As usual, she dressed in somber colors and wore a veiled hat. "Listen to what?" she asked as she took off her coat.

Henry cleared his throat, before reading the letter aloud.

*Dear Sirs,*

*I submit this letter to your publication, in hopes of generating interest in an experiment I propose to conduct. I have long held a fascination for the spirit realm, one which has only increased after the passing of my parents last year. Their transition to the Summerland has left me even more curious about those poor souls who cannot seem to find rest, and instead linger on our side of the veil.*

*As a result, I propose to make the most thorough investigation of a haunted site ever undertaken. I intend to gather mediums of several types, each with his or her own area of expertise, who will work together to investigate the phenomenon. It is my hope the extensive gathering of knowledge will yield a depth of understanding a single medium would not be able to achieve.*

*I have already secured the site for the investigation. Angel's Shadow Orphanage, located in the township of Angel Mountain, West Virginia, is infamous in local legend, but less known to the outside world.*

*Any mediums interested in joining are asked to write to me at the address below. All applicants will be thoroughly interviewed and must present no less than three references of good character. Payment generous.*

*Yours truly,*
*Mr. Charles Thorpe*

"Payment generous," Henry repeated. Surely this would be just the thing to divert Lizzie and Vincent from their obsession over Dunne. And if it added a bit of cash to their rather paltry bank account, so much the better. "I think we should…"

He trailed off as he looked up. Lizzie's pale face had gone utterly white. Vincent's lips were parted, and he'd grabbed at one of the display cabinets, as for support.

"Is…is something wrong?" Henry asked, baffled.

"Angel's Shadow," Lizzie said, but her voice was only a ghost of its usual self. "Vincent, it's…"

He nodded. "Yes. It's the orphanage Dunne and Ortensi were raised in."

"It's a sign," Vincent said fervently. He paced back and forth, hands clasped behind his back, his heart racing with a mix of dread and excitement. "It must be."

"It isn't a sign," Henry objected as he entered from the back room, carrying a tray laden with steaming cups of tea. "It's a coincidence. And an unfortunate one," he added dourly.

Vincent stopped his pacing. "What do you mean? Going back to where Dunne came from...it might be just what we need."

"Vincent is right," Jo said. She took one of the tea cups and brought it to Vincent. "Here. Sit down with Lizzie."

Lizzie sat at the table where they usually did quick readings for clients who didn't want a full séance upstairs. Henry set the tea before her, but she only stared at it, as if she'd never seen a cup before. Vincent started toward the empty chair, but the energy crackling along his nerves demanded an outlet. Instead, he took a sip of hot tea, sweetened with honey, put the cup on the table, and began to pace again.

"It's unfortunate because you've let this business with Dunne take over your lives." Henry stepped deliberately in front of Vincent. With the curtains of the store still drawn, the only light came from the gas lamps. They gleamed off the gold rim of Henry's spectacles, reflected from the glass to hide his eyes. "I was hoping to find something new for you to concentrate on. Instead, I seem to have made things worse."

Vincent frowned. "I thought you wanted to help us," he said, trying and failing to keep the hurt from his voice.

"I do!" Henry grabbed Vincent's hands, tightening his grip when Vincent immediately tried to pull away. "Love, please. Listen to me for a minute. I want you to be happy. More than anything. At first I thought this search would bring you some kind of peace. But it's only made you more miserable with every passing day."

Vincent relented, twining his fingers with Henry's. "I know you want to look out for us. But..."

"You don't understand, Henry," Lizzie said at last. She reached for her cup, but only held it in her hands. "Dunne wasn't just our mentor. He saved our lives. He *loved* us. So did Sylvester Ortensi. To find out, after all this time, that he'd lied to us, that he'd chosen us because he knew we'd be loyal, because we'd do anything without question..."

Tears thickened her voice, and she put a hand to her eyes. Vincent let go of Henry and went to her. Dragging the chair around, he sat down and wrapped an arm around her shoulders. "He taught us more than just how to be mediums," he said, meeting Henry's gaze. "He taught us to be decent people. And part of that is honoring our obligations."

"I'd say he was the one with obligations to you, given his behavior," Henry snapped.

"I don't mean obligations to Dunne." Vincent squeezed Lizzie's shoulder comfortingly. "Ortensi clearly believed the Grand Harmonium could be used for evil."

Henry sniffed. "As the man tried to murder me, I can't say I think much of his opinion on the subject of good versus evil. Besides, without the Astral Key, the Harmonium doesn't work."

"Doesn't work, or doesn't work as intended?" Jo asked. "He seemed awfully concerned about what you might do with it, Henry."

"Jo's right," Vincent said. "If it could be used by those with bad intentions, then it's Lizzie and my responsibility to find it before anyone else does."

"It isn't your responsibility," Henry objected.

"Dunne was our mentor," Lizzie said simply. "If he and Ortensi put something dangerous into the world, it falls to us to make it right."

Henry took off his spectacles and rubbed at his eyes. "Even so, what sort of answers could you possibly hope to find in this orphanage? Creating some sort of device or machine to communicate with the dead, or even to return them to haunt this world, seems a bit advanced for children."

"Ortensi said his youth was gone and implied other people had been somehow involved with the Grand Harmonium. Or at least this 'Arabella.'" Vincent said. He let his arm fall, now that Lizzie had regained her composure. "Dunne and Ortensi apprenticed together, but it was a bit unusual. They'd both been orphans, like us." Well, Lizzie wasn't strictly an orphan, but as her family had mistreated her, she might as well have been. "Their mentor decided to open an orphanage founded on the principles of the Spiritualist movement, which was still in its early years. Dunne said everything he'd learned about aiding others—about caring for both the living and the dead—he learned from her. She may have had a connection to the Grand Harmonium, or at least laid the foundation it was constructed on. Perhaps Arabella was another apprentice."

"And what happened to the orphanage?" Henry asked. "How did it come to be haunted?"

"He didn't say." Lizzie shrugged and sipped her tea. "He mentioned his mentor had passed across the veil many years ago, but nothing more specific. I didn't think to ask."

"I simply assumed the orphanage closed upon her death," Vincent added. God, why had he never questioned Dunne more thoroughly?

There hadn't seemed any need, though. Dunne had spoken fondly of his mentor, gotten a faraway look on his face, and let them draw their own conclusions. Why would either of them have thought to interrogate him on the details?

"Perhaps it did," Henry said. "Just because the locals believe the building is haunted doesn't mean anything. The legend probably grew up because of the spiritualist connection."

"We have to find out." Vincent glanced at Lizzie. She nodded in agreement. "I'm sorry, Henry. I know you're worried this will only make things worse somehow. But if there's the possibility we might learn more about the Grand Harmonium, no matter how slim, we have to take it."

"And if there are no answers?" Henry asked softly. "If the dead of the orphanage are just as silent as Dunne has been?"

"If the Grand Harmonium poses any danger to either the living or the dead, we have to find it," Vincent said simply. "Or at least try. But this experiment of Mr. Thorpe's—the fact he's chosen Angel's Shadow, and decided to advertise in the very journal we subscribe to—it's not merely a coincidence, Henry. It can't be. Some higher power, some spirit, guided his hand."

Henry's lips thinned. Though he didn't say anything, Vincent could tell he wasn't convinced.

"I'll write to this Mr. Thorpe." Lizzie seemed to have entirely recovered from her shock. "I'm sure I can convince him to accept us. If nothing else, there are very few clairgustants around, which should be to our advantage."

"Not to mention the scientific apparatus we can bring to bear," Henry added.

Vincent's heart gave a foolish little lurch. "You mean to come with us? I thought you disapproved."

"I'm concerned." Henry's blue gaze found his and held it. "But we're a...a team, I suppose. If any of us go, all of us go."

"Exactly," Jo said with a nod. "One for all, and all for one." Henry arched a brow at her, and she shrugged. "What? Dad loved that book."

# CHAPTER 3

LESS THAN TWO weeks later, Vincent stared out the window as their train pulled in to Angel Mountain.

There wasn't a great deal to the town, so far as he could tell. A modest depot, a scattering of houses, and a few larger buildings set away from the tracks. Mountains rose all around them, their thickly wooded sides the dull gray of barren branches beneath a cloudy November sky. Patches of gray stone showed here and there on the slopes, the bones of the earth breaking through to the surface.

"I bet it was beautiful a couple of weeks ago before all the leaves fell," Jo said, leaning over him to peer out.

"If you like this sort of thing." Dunne had lived in New York City when they'd met him, as far as one could get from this wild, rugged landscape. "Why do we keep going places with so much *nature* around? I imagine there's not a decent café in a hundred miles."

"This was your idea," Henry reminded him as they rose and began to gather their things.

"Proof no one should ever listen to me," Vincent drawled. "I blame Lizzie. She shouldn't have been so convincing in her letter."

Naturally, the letter had just been the beginning. Thorpe had wanted references and details of their equipment. Their correspondence had been almost daily, and Lizzie said he seemed genuinely excited by the prospect of utilizing Henry's talents as well as theirs.

They'd debated telling him about their connection to the orphanage. Henry had been in favor of laying their cards on the table from the start. But the Grand Harmonium had already driven Ortensi to dabble in necromancy. To try and kill them all, when they moved to prevent him.

They might find no clues to the Harmonium at the orphanage. But if they did, and Thorpe learned of it alongside them, what action might he take? They didn't know the man, couldn't guess at his character.

Vincent had thought he knew Ortensi. Knew Dunne. They'd both believed the Grand Harmonium worth killing for—or at least, risking apprentices for, in Dunne's case. There was no telling what this Thorpe fellow might do.

In the end, Henry had let their argument persuade him. They would remain silent on the subject of Dunne and Ortensi, at least in front of Thorpe and the other mediums he'd collected.

As they descended onto the platform, a strikingly handsome man stepped forward to greet them. A silk top hat crowned his thick black hair, and his dove gray suit was of excellent cut and quality. Vincent tried, unsuccessfully, to tell himself the fashion was far too sober, and there was no reason whatsoever to be jealous of the man's clothes.

"Mr. Strauss?" he asked Henry, who was in the forefront. "Permit me to introduce myself. I'm Charles Thorpe, your host for the next few days. I'm so thrilled you could come."

Henry shook his hand. "Thank you, sir. We're very glad to be here. Allow me to present my partners, Miss Elizabeth Devereaux and Mr. Vincent Night, and my cousin and assistant, Miss Jocelyn Strauss."

Thorpe's hazel eyes fixed on Lizzie, and his lips parted slightly. "I... that is, it is my greatest pleasure to at last meet you in person, Miss Devereaux." He bowed over her gloved hand. "I very much enjoyed our correspondence."

Lizzie seemed a bit taken aback. "You're most kind."

"Not at all." He shook Vincent's hand, then bowed over Jo's. If he found anything objectionable about their races, he gave no indication. "Please, allow my men to take your luggage, and accompany me in my coach to the house I've rented for our stay."

"Some of our equipment is quite delicate," Henry said uncertainly.

"I've instructed them to be exceedingly careful," Thorpe reassured him. "Though if you prefer to supervise the unloading yourself, you are of course welcome to do so. The ladies, Mr. Night, and I can retire to the house, then send the coach back for you."

"Come along, Henry," Vincent said. "Your instruments have

survived similar trips with no harm, as you well know."

"I suppose." Henry followed them through the depot, though not without a number of backward glances in the direction of the baggage car.

Thorpe led the way to a well-appointed coach. He assisted Lizzie and Jo inside, before climbing in himself. Vincent and Henry took the rear-facing seat across from them.

"The coach is lovely," Lizzie said as they started off. Vincent suspected they were both thinking along the same lines. Thorpe clearly had money to spare; if they could impress him over the next few days, perhaps he would consider hiring them again the next time he wished to make an investigation.

"Thank you. It originally belonged to my parents."

"Our condolences on the loss," Henry added.

Thorpe's smile turned sad. "I admit I miss them both a great deal. I was their only child—adopted, as it happens. Which was one of the reasons I found myself drawn to the orphanage, having had experiences myself in such an institute, though I was very small at the time." He paused, looking out the window. "My father was Ulysses Thorpe—you may have heard of the baking powder he developed? Mother had a head for business, and between the two of them, they built a small company. When it came time to retire, they sold it to a competitor for…well, I'm sure someone like Mr. Vanderbilt would consider it to be mere pocket change, but quite enough coin for us ordinary mortals. Rather than let myself grow idle, I decided to use a portion of my inheritance to push the frontier of psychical science. As my father spent his own formative years in an orphanage as well, I believe he'd be glad I chose to conduct our experiment here."

"Now that we've arrived, can you tell us what to expect?" Lizzie asked.

"If I may beg your indulgence, I would prefer to lay out the facts of the matter after dinner," Thorpe said apologetically. "Your fellow mediums are here already, and it would be easiest to relate the story a single time for everyone."

"Of course," Lizzie said. "I quite understand."

Silence fell over them as the coach made its way through the streets. Vincent stared out at the simple houses, the small businesses. Had Dunne once walked here? Ortensi?

Perhaps. Likely they would have spent most of their time at the orphanage as children. Dunne had never mentioned returning here as an adult; perhaps he was glad to have put it behind him.

Had he even known the orphanage was rumored to be haunted? Surely if he had, he would have come to lay the dead to rest. Especially if he had known some of them in life.

Wouldn't he?

With any luck, they would find some sort of answers here. If they didn't…

Suppressing a sigh, he turned back to the window. As they passed what appeared to be the general store, the old men seated outside hastily averted their gazes. All but one, anyway, who defiantly made a sign against evil in their direction.

Henry had spotted it, too. "The locals don't seem pleased to see us."

"No." Thorpe's mouth twitched. "The orphanage is rumored to be cursed."

"Cursed *and* haunted." Vincent raised a brow. "Quite the reputation."

"I don't believe in curses," Thorpe said. "But Angel Mountain is remote, and its people cling to tradition and superstition alike. I was forced to hire servants from Roanoke and bring them with me, once the locals discovered my business." He shifted slightly in his seat. "But here we are."

The house Thorpe had rented would be better described as a mansion, four stories tall, clad in pale stone, its windows shining with lights as the short November day raced toward twilight. A footman opened the coach door for them. Thorpe hopped out and assisted Lizzie and Jo down. At least the fellow had good manners. Indeed, he seemed entirely pleasant, which was a nice change of pace from their employer in Devil's Walk.

Baggage arrived on their heels, and footmen hurriedly removed it from the cart and fell in behind them. "I've had rooms prepared for each of you," Thorpe said. "I'm certain you'd like to wash the dust off and rest a bit before dinner. The butler will ring the gong when it's ready." He offered them all a smile, ending with Lizzie. "Again, thank you for coming. I'm very glad to have you here."

Was it Vincent's imagination, or did a light blush stain Lizzie's cheeks? "As we are grateful for the opportunity," she murmured.

"Shall I show you to your rooms?" asked the butler.

At their assent, he led them up the grand staircase, past a crystal chandelier. Jo stared around, her eyes enormous. It was, Vincent acknowledged silently, rather overwhelming. Thorpe obviously had a great deal of money, to afford to rent such a place, along with all the servants to staff it. No doubt it was the summer house for someone important, who retreated to the mountains during the hot months, then left for New York or Boston when the cold crept in.

A maid met them at the top of the stairs. She looked surprised at the sight of Jo, but only said, "If you'll follow me this way, ladies, I'll show you to your rooms in the women's wing."

They followed her, but Jo looked back over her shoulder. *"The women's wing,"* she mouthed at them, brows rising.

*"Rich people,"* Vincent mouthed back. Henry shot them both a reproving look.

"This is your room, Mr. Night," the butler said, opening one of the doors. "And yours, Mr. Strauss."

They were next to one another, which could prove convenient. Vincent stood aside while his baggage was deposited. Once the servant was gone, he opened his trunk and began to unpack his clothing. Fortunately it appeared to have survived the trip without creasing. Even if it hadn't, the house seemed well-staffed enough to spare a maid to press a coat or two.

Once he was done, he sat down on the edge of the bed. The down mattress yielded beneath him, and with a sigh, he fell back into its embrace. He ought to see about changing for dinner, but the bed was so comfortable...

Henry's raised voice, raw with fury, echoed through the wall beside his head: "You blackguard. You *fraud.* I'll tell everyone!"

Henry washed in the basin, then put his things away. The room was far grander than anything he was used to, and he began to wonder if at least their trip might have a profitable outcome.

Not that it mattered, in comparison to finding some sort of peace for Vincent and Lizzie. He'd sensed their tension on the entire trip from Baltimore, longed to have the freedom to take Vincent's hand in his for comfort. With any luck, the orphanage would offer up some clue to allow them to find the blasted Harmonium and put an end to all this.

Judging by his writing, Ortensi believed this Grand Harmonium made communion with the dead as simple as waking one who was merely asleep. Vincent and Lizzie were willing to take the man at his word, but Henry was less certain. After all, he'd spent years perfecting the Electro-Séance. Though it could make séances easier at times, in the cases where a spirit was too weak to communicate only through a medium, or when there was some danger in contacting the ghost, there was still a great deal of effort involved. True, Ortensi had scoured the world for knowledge and materials inaccessible to Henry, but Henry would still need better proof than the writing of a madman who had tried to murder him.

Henry glanced at the bed, but his thoughts were too much in turmoil to consider napping, or even resting comfortably. He'd glimpsed a library through one of the open doors on the first floor. Perhaps it would yield up some kind of distraction.

He stepped into the hall and spotted another man making for one of the other rooms. One of the mediums they would be working with, no doubt. His brown hair shone in the gaslight, and his suit coat shaped broad shoulders. There seemed something oddly familiar about him, even from behind.

"Hello," Henry said uncertainly.

The man turned, and Henry's heart nearly stopped.

He'd last seen the face looking back at him over a decade ago. There were more lines now, and gray at the temples, but he would have known the man anywhere.

After all, he'd been the one to destroy Henry's life.

"Isaac Woodsend," Henry said, feeling as though he'd been punched in the gut. "What the hell are you doing here?"

Woodsend sauntered toward him, a smile on his mouth. "Well, well. If it isn't little Henry Strauss." His eyes raked Henry's form. "Not so little now, it seems."

Nausea clawed at Henry's throat. "You blackguard. You *fraud*. I'll tell everyone—"

"What your father did to my family?" Woodsend asked with an arched brow.

The words made no sense. "My—my father?"

Woodsend gestured to Henry's door. "Perhaps we should speak of this in private."

The thought of being alone with the man made Henry's skin crawl with revulsion. He'd been such a fool when Woodsend appeared on the doorstep of his childhood home, claiming to have received a message from Henry's father from beyond the grave.

A young fool, ready to believe. Henry had received a visitation from Father himself, shortly after the funeral. He even had proof the apparition had been real and not a dream, in the form of an emerald stickpin Father had been buried with, apported into Henry's room.

Woodsend had been so handsome, so sophisticated, Henry couldn't help but be flattered by his attentions. But their illicit relationship left him with only shame and a sense of wrongness, even before the man made off with the last of the Strauss fortune.

"Isaac Woodsend was a false identity, as I'm sure you guessed. My real name is Ira Wellington." Woodsend—Wellington—cocked his head. "Sound familiar?"

Henry started to deny it—then stopped. "Wellington…Father had a friend by the name. He died when I was young."

Wellington's expression darkened. "Because Alfred Strauss betrayed him."

Henry's heart thudded against his ribs. "Fine. We'll speak in my room."

Wellington preceded him. Henry started to shut the door, but the memory of all the other closed doors they'd been behind stayed his hand. Instead, he pushed it nearly to, leaving a crack open to the hallway.

"What are you blathering on about?" he demanded. "Or is this another of your lies? If you were one of the Wellingtons, why didn't Mother recognize you?"

"We'd never met." Wellington seated himself on the bed. "I'd left for university before the family moved to Baltimore. After, my studies took me to Europe. I was on my way back to the states, when I heard my father died by his own hand."

Henry desperately searched his memory. He'd been only a child, perhaps eleven or twelve at the most, when Mr. Wellington had died. He dimly recalled the funeral, but no more. "My father had nothing to do with his death."

"Didn't he though? Alfred sold my father worthless railroad stock at inflated prices. When the panic of '73 came along, he lost *everything*."

"Father would never have done such a thing!" Henry exclaimed. "He was a good man—an honorable man!"

"Then why did he sell off all his stock just before the panic? He was president of a bank; he must have known collapse was on the horizon. So he convinced my father it was a safe investment, sold it to him at exorbitant prices, and walked away." Wellington's expression hardened. "I was forced to return from Europe because there was nothing left to fund my scholarship. By the time I arrived home, Father was dead and the rest of the family moved in with an aunt in New York. Our house gone, any hopes of my younger brothers going to university evaporated. Mother said she'd overheard Father pleading with Alfred to use the bank's resources to cushion the blow, but he refused. The next day, Father hung himself in despair."

Henry leaned against the wall. He'd never heard any of this. "Father couldn't have used the bank's money to save your father from his own bad investments."

"It was Alfred's fault he'd made those investments to begin with," Wellington replied bitterly. "When I heard what had happened, I swore he would pay. But he died before I could exact revenge. So I did something even better. I helped myself to the money he should have shared with my father in the first place. I used it to drag my family out of the poverty to which he'd consigned them."

Money wasn't the only thing he'd helped himself to. Henry's shoulders ached, the muscles tight as wires. "You utter villain. You cost us our place in society, our home, *everything*. Mother died in a drafty apartment we shared with two other families. It took me years to rebuild even a tenth of what you stole. I ought to thrash you within an inch of your life!"

"Do it, and Thorpe will throw you out into the street. Or be sensible, and you'll reclaim everything you once had, and more." Wellington smiled, but the expression sent a shiver down Henry's spine. "I'll admit, I was taken aback when I discovered Thorpe was considering hiring you. I intended to persuade him to hire someone else, but once I saw your qualifications, I realized you might be of considerable use. You're quite a clever boy, aren't you, Henry?"

"Go to hell," Henry snapped. "Once Thorpe learns you're nothing but a fraud, he'll cast you into the street."

"Ah, but I'm not a fraud." Wellington leaned back casually, causing the bed to creak beneath him. "Just because I wasn't truthful with you hardly means I have no psychical talent. I have proven myself to Mr. Thorpe—I've worked with him for months, as a matter of fact. We've become good friends. Whereas you are merely someone who answered an advertisement in a journal."

Wellington couldn't be an actual medium. This had to be yet one more lie. "I don't believe you."

"You'll see. And once you do, consider working together. Such an alliance will be *very* beneficial, financially." Wellington smoothed his hand deliberately over the comforter. "There are other potential benefits as well, of course."

Vincent cleared his throat from the doorway.

# CHAPTER 4

**WELLINGTON HASTILY STOOD.** Vincent shoved the door open all the way and leaned against the frame, his hips cocked. He wore a lazy expression that might have deceived Wellington, but his black eyes were cold and hard as chips of anthracite.

Wellington's lip curled. "What do you mean by spying on us? Have you no sense of decency whatsoever?"

"More of it than is probably healthy." Vincent removed himself from the doorframe and sauntered to Henry's side. "Vincent Night, at your service. Spirit medium and Henry's...partner."

Henry wanted to seize Vincent's hand. But not in front of Wellington. "Vincent, this is a fraud and liar who is currently going by Ira Wellington."

"So charming to meet you," Vincent said, in a voice suggesting the exact opposite. "I can't wait to see your mediumship tomorrow."

Henry's heart stuttered. "What do you mean? We have to—"

"Let him hoist himself on his own petard? How very clever of you, Henry." Vincent's smile showed too many teeth to be friendly. "Mr. Wellington, your claims to mediumship are as false as they ever were. You can't hope to continue your fraud, not in the company of actual spirit mediums, let alone Henry's instruments. I suggest you take your leave while you still have the chance. I'm sure you've had plenty of practice when it comes to slinking away in the dead of night."

Wellington's expression had become fixed...but now it eased into a smirk. "I have nothing to fear, Mr. Night. As I've told our Henry—"

"I wouldn't repeat that particular phrase, were I you," Vincent murmured.

To Henry's surprise, Wellington glanced down. "As I informed Mr. Strauss, I have a genuine talent. You'll see for yourself soon enough, so dragging up past events will only make you look bad in Charles's—I mean, Mr. Thorpe's—eyes." Wellington had regained his smirk. "I'll see you both at dinner."

He started out, but Henry called. "You stole my father's stickpin. I should like it back."

Wellington paused. "Long sold, dear boy, so don't think to see it again."

The moment he was gone, Vincent crossed the room and shut the door firmly behind him. "Are you all right, Henry?"

Henry sank down on the edge of the bed. "I'm not sure." The aftermath of shock and anger left him feeling vaguely ill, his stomach unsettled, his muscles weak. "I'd never expected to see him again."

"The man is a cockroach, scuttling out from under the furniture." Vincent sat beside him. "He won't stay long in the light."

"He won't just creep away." Henry swallowed. "He's been helping—or, I suppose, deceiving—Thorpe for months. He's Thorpe's partner in this. And the accusations he made against my father..."

Vincent took his hand. "Could they be true?"

"No." Henry stared down at their joined fingers. Vincent had such beautiful hands, the fingers long and dark. Graceful, against Henry's thick, scarred digits. "Father would never have sold stock he knew was about to become worthless. The railroads had been booming ever since the end of the war; why would he imagine anything would change? I suppose Wellington's mother wanted something to blame other than bad luck and bad timing." Henry drew a ragged breath. "I can't believe...it was bad enough when I thought Woodsend had just been a fraud. But to know our fathers had been friends, to realize there was deliberate malice behind everything he did to us...to me..."

"Do you wish to leave?" Vincent asked quietly.

He wanted to say yes. Leave. The thought of being in proximity with Wellington, of working with him, turned Henry's stomach. But... "You'd remain here. I'd be leaving you behind."

Vincent hesitated visibly. "I wouldn't want to. But you heard what Wellington said. He offered you financial benefits in return for your cooperation." The copper column of his throat worked as he swallowed. "I can only assume he meant beyond what Mr. Thorpe has already promised to pay us."

A chill shocked down Henry's spine. He'd been so flustered at being confronted with Wellington's presence, he'd let that detail slip past him. "Surely he wasn't referring to the Grand Harmonium. Ortensi and Dunne didn't even tell you about it; they wouldn't have trusted anyone else."

Vincent's look was grim. "Mr. Thorpe mentioned his father was in an orphanage. Perhaps Ortensi and Dunne weren't the only apprentices."

"Then the choice of Angel's Shadow may not have been as innocent as Mr. Thorpe made it sound," Henry said slowly. "Dear God."

"We don't know that for certain," Vincent cautioned. "I don't want to jump to wild conclusions and assume Mr. Thorpe is anything other than he appears. But the possibility exists he knows about the Harmonium and wishes to exploit it in some fashion, as Ortensi feared you would."

"And knowing that, we can't afford to leave," Henry said. He straightened his shoulders. "I'll face Wellington for as long as it takes. Surely, whatever Thorpe's motives for coming here, once he realizes Wellington is a fraud, he'll give the scoundrel the boot."

"You don't have to stay," Vincent said. "If you'd rather return to Baltimore, believe me, I understand. After Dunne found me, there were certain streets in New York I'd never set foot on again, to avoid the memories."

Emotion tightened Henry's throat. "I love you. I won't abandon you, especially not when there's any possibility Thorpe is other than he seems."

Vincent's dark eyes softened. "My Henry," he whispered, threading his fingers through Henry's hair.

He tugged Vincent closer, pressed a kiss to his lips. Vincent kissed him back with such tenderness it made his chest ache.

Henry rested his head against Vincent's shoulder. "Wellington must be lying about having real talent. He'll surely expose himself if he goes with us to the orphanage. All we have to do is honestly report our own findings, and Thorpe will see the truth."

"Indeed." Vincent kissed Henry's forehead. "Maybe we'll get truly lucky, and Thorpe will have him hauled off by the police."

Henry smiled. "Now that is a cheerful thought."

~ * ~

Vincent spent most of dinner dividing his attention between Wellington and Henry. The utter gall of the swine, to speak to Henry about "other benefits" after what he'd done, set Vincent's blood to boiling. And the look in Henry's eyes afterward…

With any luck, Wellington would be on his way out of town by this time tomorrow. A shame Thorpe didn't seem the type of man to deliver a thrashing as additional punishment.

When they assembled for dinner, Thorpe introduced the last of the mediums he'd gathered, in the person of one Miss Abigail Blake. She was perhaps a few years older than Vincent and Lizzie, though younger than Wellington, and struck him as a bright and cheerful sort.

"I'm from Boston," she said, shaking hands all around as a man would do. The faint smell of tobacco wafted from her. "You won't have heard of me, I'm sure, but I'm a clairvoyant. I can see ghosts—not all the time, but before they've gathered enough energy to be visible to anyone else."

"Fascinating," Henry said, a bit too enthusiastically. He kept his back deliberately turned on Wellington. "I'd love to hear all about it over dinner. Do you know much about the electromagnetic spectrum, Miss Blake?"

"This is exactly the sort of cooperation I hope we can all show going forward." Thorpe practically beamed. Perhaps Vincent and Henry had been paranoid in assuming he had anything to hide. "You and your compatriots have Miss Blake to thank for your presence, Mr. Strauss."

Henry frowned slightly. "We do?"

"Mr. Wellington was hired first, of course," Blake said. "When I joined, Mr. Thorpe was still looking for at least one more medium to add to the company. As we spoke, I suddenly had an overwhelming feeling— a very positive one—that he should search in the Baltimore area." She shrugged one shoulder. "The spirits seldom guide me in such a way, but when they do…well, I've learned to listen."

Vincent exchanged a glance with Lizzie. He'd felt from the beginning that the letter in the journal had been a sign. And now it seemed he'd been right.

The pulse beating in his throat quickened. Even though they'd achieved no direct contact with Dunne, perhaps he had been reaching out after all. Guiding them to this place.

They were going to find answers here, if not the Grand Harmonium itself. He knew it.

The butler swung open the doors to the dining room. Thorpe

offered Lizzie his arm. "Miss Devereaux, may I escort you?"

Her smile was brighter than the gaslights. "It would be my pleasure, Mr. Thorpe."

Vincent offered his arm to Jo, who happened to be standing nearby. Miss Blake strode after them, unaccompanied. Henry trailed after her, looking a bit uncertain as to what he ought to do, and Wellington brought up the rear.

Through a bit of careful maneuvering, Vincent managed to flank Henry with Miss Blake and Jo, while he sat beside Lizzie, with Mr. Thorpe to her right. Wellington ended up between Miss Blake and Mr. Thorpe.

No time like the present to start planting the seeds for Wellington's downfall. "Mr. Wellington, is it?" Vincent drawled as the servants poured wine. "Miss Blake has shared the nature of her gift with us, but I don't think you've mentioned your own specialty. How precisely do you commune with the spirits?"

Wellington smiled, as though nothing at all was amiss. "I'm claircognizant. I receive impressions from the spirit world."

"How convenient," Vincent said drily. Vague "impressions" delivered by spirits would ordinarily be the most difficult claim to expose, at least to some other audience.

But he and Miss Blake, assuming she in fact had real talent, would know immediately whether or not a spirit was actually about. And of course Henry would be taking measurements of his own the entire time. If all three of them consistently disagreed with Wellington about the presence of spirits, Thorpe would begin to question the man's veracity soon enough. As for Thorpe's own honesty, or lack thereof, that was a concern for later.

"Hardly convenient." Wellington picked up his fork as the first course of roast beef was laid out before them. "Claircognizance is an honor, but it comes with its burdens. My path has not been an easy one, but I am grateful the spirits found me worthy."

Henry made a sound as though he'd choked on his wine. Vincent kept all of his attention fixed on Wellington, however. "You believe we're chosen by the spirits? That mediumistic talent is granted in some fashion, rather than an accident of birth?"

"But of course." Wellington's faint smile never wavered. "Surely you don't believe your gifts come from within you, Mr. Night? The spirits choose those they deem worthy enough—enlightened enough—to carry their message to the world."

No wonder Henry had wanted to replace mediums with mechanisms when they'd first met. Wellington was so slimy he made Vincent want to take a bath just by proximity. "A question wiser minds have debated throughout history," Vincent said with a languid wave of his hand, as if to disavow such tedious thoughts.

"Quite true." Wellington paused. "But as we're sharing, surely you'll enlighten Miss Blake as to what skills you and your…partners…have to offer."

"Miss Devereaux is an accomplished spirit writer and skilled in psychometry," Vincent replied. Lizzie gave him a startled look, no doubt having expected to answer for herself. Then her expression sharpened; she knew him well enough to realize something wasn't right between him and Wellington. "As for myself, I am a trance medium, able to channel spirits directly, as well as clairgustant. But where our partnership truly shines is the marriage of traditional methods of mediumship and the scientific insights brought by Mr. Strauss."

Henry flushed bright pink. "Thank you, er, Mr. Night. But I couldn't do it without Jo."

"Miss Strauss is quite the scientist in her own right," Vincent agreed. Jo beamed at their praise.

"How fascinating!" Miss Blake exclaimed. "And what a refreshing change, to see a young woman so interested in the sciences. Please, tell us of your work, both of you."

Henry and Jo expounded through most of dinner. As they did so, Vincent caught Wellington's eye. As he'd expected, Wellington looked annoyed. Wellington struck him as the sort of man who liked to be the center of attention. By placing Henry and Jo in the spotlight, Vincent had achieved a bit of petty revenge.

Dunne would have told him not to stoop to pettiness.

Once the dessert course was finished, Thorpe rose to his feet. "Thank you all for a pleasant dinner. That was most informative, Mr. Strauss, Miss Strauss." He clasped his hands before him. "Now I suggest we retire to the library. Brandy and coffee will be served, and I shall reveal to you what I know of Angel's Shadow Orphanage…and the unquiet spirits which walk within."

Vincent sprawled in an overstuffed chair near the library's fire, brandy held loosely in his hand. Though he pretended languor, he watched Thorpe intently through his lashes for any hint of duplicity. Given the looks Thorpe and Lizzie had given one another when they thought no one else was watching, he hoped the suspicions he harbored were unfounded, and Thorpe as perfectly innocent as he'd first presented himself.

"Angel's Shadow was founded in 1844 by Mrs. Betsy Marsden." Thorpe swirled the contents of his brandy snifter. "Though her husband was officially the superintendent and she the matron, it was clear to everyone Mrs. Marsden was the one making the decisions."

"You mentioned she wished it to be run on spiritualist principles," Vincent prompted.

"Correct." Thorpe shifted forward in the chair he'd taken next to Lizzie. Jo and Henry occupied the couch, and Miss Blake leaned against the stones of the fireplace, brazenly smoking a pipe. "Mrs. Marsden claimed she had been healed by a spirit as a child, and herself had a mediumistic gift. She believed by gathering orphaned mediums together, she could nurture their talents to best advantage."

Dunne and Ortensi must have been among them. They would have been around twelve or so years of age when the orphanage opened.

"Why here?" Henry asked. "Most orphanages are nearer to larger towns, where there are more children. For what we've seen of Angel Mountain thus far, I can't imagine there was much of a town at the time, before even the railroad."

"An excellent question," Thorpe replied with an enthusiastic nod. He reminded Vincent rather strongly of an energetic puppy. Perhaps they'd been entirely wrong to doubt him; certainly he seemed honestly excited to have their assistance. "And one of the few I can answer with certainty. Any journals Mrs. Marsden might have kept are lost to time, or else somewhere within the orphanage itself. However, she corresponded regularly with other spiritualists, and I've located some of her letters. According to them, her spirit guide instructed her where to build."

Vincent and Lizzie exchanged a glance. Ortensi had found many cases of genuine spirit guides on his travels around the world, but in Vincent's personal experience, they were more often trotted out by those with little or no real talent. Indian spirit guides were something of a fashion among anyone wishing to claim a link to special wisdom or occult knowledge. And meanwhile, actual living Indians were slaughtered by the thousands in the west, and no one seemed to care.

For once, the bitterness in his mouth had nothing to do with ghosts.

"Fascinating," Lizzie murmured. "Did she mention why…it? He?… asked for such a remote location?"

"She referred to the spirit as Xabat," Thorpe said. "And the answer seems to have been two-fold. Mrs. Marsden wished to shield the children from any outside influence. She believed keeping the innate purity of youth intact would strengthen the children's affinity with the spirit realm. Inversely, corruption by the world would sully their gifts."

If that were true, Vincent would have been a poor medium indeed, barely worth training by the time Dunne found him. But he kept the opinion to himself.

"To that end," Thorpe continued, "the children were kept within the walls of the orphanage grounds at all times. Nor was any contact allowed with the outside world. No letters, no newspapers, nothing which might disturb their serenity."

"So they were prisoners," Lizzie said.

"In a way, yes." A flicker of sorrow passed over Thorpe's face, and Vincent wondered if he recalled his own experiences in such an institution. A moment later, his cheerful demeanor had returned. "Mrs. Marsden also believed certain places in the world were naturally closer to the spirit realm. She claimed the spirit guide led her here because Angel Mountain had some unusual property which made it easier to contact the other side."

"All very interesting, but what about the haunting?" Miss Blake asked. "That is what we're here for, isn't it?"

Lizzie cast her a cool gaze. "Knowing the full history of the building can only be to our advantage."

Thorpe had blushed slightly when Miss Blake spoke, but seemed bolstered by Lizzie's comment. "Such was my intent, Miss Devereaux. But I shouldn't wish to linger too long over unimportant details."

Vincent bit back a curse. Such details might hold some vital clue as to Dunne's past, or the Grand Harmonium.

Or give some hint as to how much Thorpe might know about either one.

"Angel's Shadow came to an unfortunate, and rather abrupt, end." Thorpe turned his gaze to the fire, as if contemplating the sorrows of the past in its flames. "Only five years after it was completed, something very strange happened. Though the children were forbidden to come into town, naturally the adults visited to place orders with the general store, or to secure fresh food and milk from the community farmers. When they failed to appear as usual, the owner of the dairy sent one of his boys with the milk, on the assumption the matter had simply been forgotten. But no one answered his calls from outside the gates. At length he ventured inside and found the place abandoned."

"So they left?" Jo asked. "Without telling anyone?"

"Therein lies the mystery. According to the boy—who now runs a farm of his own a valley over—everything had been left in place. Clothing, food, toys, personal articles…all remained, as though the children and their wardens had simply stepped out for a few moments." Thorpe's chair creaked as he leaned back. "He went for help, and a party of men searched the woods, in case the orphanage's inhabitants had in fact gone for a walk to take in the mountain air, only to have some mishap befall them. But they found no trace. It was as though everyone who had lived in the orphanage slipped through a crack in the world and vanished."

Jo shivered. "How extraordinary," Miss Blake said. "I suppose stories grew up around it afterward?"

Was it Vincent's imagination, or did a shadow pass over Thorpe's expression? "Told only in whispers, and with great reluctance—or so I learned when I tried to question anyone who had been alive at the time. The farmer's boy, a few others. One widow confided her husband had gone inside as a boy and been attacked by some invisible force." All Thorpe's earlier energy had drained away. "Otherwise, I heard only the usual stories about lights seen in the window, by travelers who were always some distance away. If anyone knew more, they never told." He seemed to realize his slump and rallied visibly. "So when the idea of gathering mediums to work together occurred to me, it seemed a good place to investigate. I bought the property at auction, and, well, here we are."

Vincent kept his face neutral, but frowned mentally. Thorpe's explanation seemed a bit thin. Surely there were plenty of more easily accessible haunted places to investigate. He knew of half a dozen in Baltimore alone, which wouldn't have required a long train ride and renting an entire mansion. Let alone buying the haunted property outright.

Surely Thorpe knew of the Grand Harmonium. Why Angel's Shadow had been abandoned so abruptly, Vincent couldn't imagine, but Ortensi and Dunne at least had departed and lived out the rest of their lives elsewhere. Perhaps others had as well.

"So tomorrow we go to the orphanage and see what we can find?" Vincent asked, keeping his face neutral.

"Exactly," Thorpe said. "Now, I suggest we all retire to bed and get some sleep. First thing tomorrow, we'll pay a visit to the ghosts."

# CHAPTER 5

"**IRA WELLINGTON IS** Isaac Woodsend?" Jo's eyes narrowed in fury. "You have to tell Mr. Thorpe at once! Then Vincent can give him a good thrashing."

Henry's face heated with embarrassment. "Really, Jo, have you been reading those romantic novels again?"

Vincent raised a languid brow where he stood leaning against the wall beside the door. They'd waited until the rest of the house fell silent, before gathering in Henry's room. Henry perched on the edge of the bed, Jo beside him, while Lizzie took the chair.

"I'm not precisely the thrashing type," Vincent said dryly.

"Even so, we should tell Mr. Thorpe." Lizzie straightened her skirts. "He won't wish to be partnered with such a blackguard."

"Perhaps." Vincent inspected his fingernails carefully. "But not only have they been working together for months, where we are the newcomers…I rather think Mr. Thorpe is hiding something."

Henry eagerly seized on any excuse to change the topic from his past. Sitting across from Wellington at dinner had been a sort of torture, though at least the discussion of his equipment and methods had allowed him to focus on something else. "Wellington did imply if I kept quiet about his fraudulent past, there would be monetary rewards at the end. And I don't think he just meant the fee Thorpe has agreed to pay us."

Lizzie frowned. "Why would Mr. Thorpe hide something? He's the one who brought us here in the first place. There'd be no point."

"Perhaps the same reason we're hiding things?" Vincent suggested. "He knows about the Grand Harmonium?"

"Preposterous!" Lizzie exclaimed. Vincent arched a brow at her, and she unaccountably flushed crimson. "That is, Mr. Thorpe has never struck me as a duplicitous man. His correspondence betrayed nothing more than a spirit of honest inquiry."

"I'm sure it did," Vincent murmured. "I did notice you ceased to share those letters with us after the first few exchanges."

Lizzie shot him a murderous look. "If we spoke of personal matters, it's hardly your concern, Vincent Night."

"Mr. Thorpe said he had letters from Mrs. Marsden. Maybe they mention the Grand Harmonium?" Jo suggested. She bounced a little on the bed, until Henry shot her a quelling glance. "Lizzie could ask him if we can read the letters ourselves."

Lizzie brightened. "That's not a bad idea. Assuming he has them, and didn't simply read them before giving them back. I'll inquire over breakfast."

"What do you think happened?" Jo asked. "At the orphanage, I mean. No bodies were ever found, but it's assumed everyone died. But we know Ortensi and Dunne at least survived."

"Perhaps no one died?" Henry suggested, echoing Vincent's earlier thought. "Just because the locals have stories about the mysteriously abandoned orphanage doesn't mean it's actually haunted, after all. It's possible they all simply left and never returned, for reasons we can't guess at."

"Then this will be a very short investigation," Lizzie said. "Presumably Mr. Wellington will receive 'impressions from the spirits' or some such rot, but—assuming Miss Blake is genuine—the rest of us will find nothing. Still, we should take the opportunity to go through the place as thoroughly as possible. Even if we can't discover why it was abandoned, we may yet learn something."

"And even if all our speculations are groundless, and we don't learn anything, we'll still get paid," Henry added.

"What if Mr. Thorpe does know something concerning the Grand Harmonium?" Jo asked. "Or stumbles over it in the orphanage? Do we try to join forces with him?"

"We'll have to decide later, once we have a better idea of his character," Vincent said. Lizzie opened her mouth, then shut it again. "Mr. Thorpe is a man of business. He might be tempted to use it for his own ends."

"As Ortensi feared I would do," Henry muttered. Given the depths Ortensi had stooped to, the assessment shouldn't have stung. "The orphanage is Mr. Thorpe's property—technically whatever is found on it belongs to him. If the Grand Harmonium is here, that doesn't bode well for us."

"Mr. Thorpe isn't a man of business," Lizzie said, looking vexed. "His father was. Mr. Thorpe sold the company to do other things."

"Other things being investigate a haunted orphanage." Vincent waved an impatient hand at her. "Even if you're right, he might sell off the Grand Harmonium as well."

"Who owned the property before?" Jo asked.

Henry straightened. "A very good question, Jo. It recently came up to auction, suggesting the previous owner died."

"Or went bankrupt," Vincent said uneasily. "But I take your meaning. You think Ortensi owned it."

"Dunne and Ortensi dedicated their lives to this Harmonium. If there's some connection to the orphanage, surely they wouldn't have taken the chance on anyone else claiming or destroying it."

"It's late," Lizzie said, rising to her feet. "And we've nothing but speculation at the moment. We'll know more after we see the orphanage tomorrow. Though I do suggest at least one of us stay with Mr. Thorpe at all times while exploring the place, just in case he does come across some clue." She let out a long sigh. "I hate to think he's concealing anything from us...but I trust your instincts, Vincent."

He gave her a little bow. "Thank you."

"We'll see you in the morning. Come along, Jo, let's sneak back to the women's wing, before anyone realizes we're having private consultations away from the rest of the group."

They said their goodnights, and the ladies slipped out. Vincent lingered, though.

"Would you like to stay for a while?" Henry asked. He'd grown used to waking up beside Vincent, and the thought his lover would have to leave before dawn brought an expected ache to his chest. It seemed foolish; he'd waked alone for most of his life, save for the last few months.

Vincent's pensive look slipped away, replaced by a smile. "Would you like me to?" He paused, glancing in the direction of the hall. "I worried seeing Wellington again might bring back unkind memories."

"Of course it did. But he has nothing to do with us."

Vincent sat beside him, the mattress dipping under his weight. Long, sensitive fingers cupped Henry's jaw. "I love you, Henry. If I accomplish nothing else in Angel's Shadow, I'll prove the man a fraud and have him cast out, I swear it."

Emotion tangled into a knot Henry didn't try to unravel. Anger and grief and the memory of first love, of humiliation and betrayal. He shoved it aside impatiently, gripping Vincent's lapels and hauling him closer. "I don't want to talk about him," he said against Vincent's lips. "I don't want to talk at all."

Vincent kissed him, gently at first, until Henry bit at his lips. Henry didn't need tenderness at the moment; he needed to forget. To lose himself in passion.

They disrobed hastily, shivering a little in the cool air. The bedrooms had fireplaces, but Henry had let the fire burn down into coals, and the fall chill had crept inside. He pulled Vincent down on top of him, wrapping his legs around Vincent's hips, kissing his throat. Vincent grabbed the heavy comforter and dragged it over them both.

"Henry," Vincent whispered, voice thick with desire. His cock lay heavy and hard against Henry's belly. Henry twisted, tried to rut against him.

"Bugger me." Henry's pulse crashed in his ears. "Please."

"Whatever you need, sweetheart."

It wasn't their normal fashion. Vincent preferred to receive, and Henry was ordinarily happy to oblige him. But they had changed things up once or twice, for the sake of experimentation.

Tonight, though…Henry wanted to forget, to stop thinking long enough to sleep. He needed Vincent's weight on him, to viscerally feel he had someone who loved him and wouldn't let him go.

Vincent slid off of him to fetch the petroleum jelly. Henry rolled over onto his belly, stuffing pillows under his hips. He gripped the sheets, anticipation thrilling through his belly, his prick aching with need.

Vincent kissed the back of his neck, the space between his shoulders, and down his spine. The blankets formed a warm tent around them, and Vincent's hands were tender. Henry bucked his hips impatiently. It earned him a throaty chuckle.

"So anxious," Vincent chided him.

"I just need you."

"I know, love." Another kiss. "Have me, then."

Henry closed his eyes when Vincent breached him. Lust and pleasure tightened his throat, and he had to remind himself to breathe.

"How is it?" Vincent asked, a trace of worry in his voice.

"Wonderful." Henry let out a long breath. "Vincent, please."

Vincent draped himself over Henry's back. He stretched out his arms, fingers interlacing with Henry's. The gesture felt strangely intimate, somehow even more so than the cock currently in his ass. Vincent groaned his name, then finally, finally, began to move.

Henry gasped and squeezed Vincent's fingers tighter. This was what he'd craved. The familiar scent of musk and citrus in his nose, the weight of his lover pushing him into the bedding, the gasps of their breath. Vincent's prick hit just the right spot with each thrust, sending shocks of pleasure through Henry, building and building. Henry gave himself up to it, nothing but raw senses, no other awareness save the bubble of warmth and pleasure and love surrounding him.

The friction of the sheets against his cock wasn't enough, so he pushed back against Vincent. Vincent let out a grunt of pleasure, moved faster, bodies shoving together more and more urgently.

"Yes," Henry babbled. "Yes, there, Vincent—"

He shuddered, arching up against Vincent's weight. Lights flashed behind his eyes and he spent helplessly into the sheets.

"Oh God," Vincent groaned. His fingers tightened on Henry's, knuckles going pale. A quick thrust, then another, and he shivered hard against Henry's back.

Silence wrapped around them like yet another blanket, woven of contentment. Vincent kissed the back of Henry's neck again and withdrew with a sigh. Henry rolled onto his side and pressed his face into Vincent's chest. Vincent stroked his hair idly.

"Feeling better?" he asked.

"Yes." Henry nuzzled closer. "Stay for a while."

"I will." Vincent's arms wound around him. "For as long as you need me."

Deep in the night, Vincent woke suddenly.

For a moment, he didn't know what had waked him, or even where he was. The unfamiliar contours of the room, the weight of Henry's body in his arms...

The taste of cigars and a well-cooked steak in his mouth.

A ghost.

Vincent froze, senses straining, heart thundering. He'd meant to go back to his room, so they hadn't bothered salting the windows and doors. Instead, they'd fallen asleep.

And now something was in the room with them.

He took a deep breath, forced back panic. The flavor in his mouth was unfamiliar—not a spirit he'd encountered before. The taste was strangely wholesome. Solid. Not the spirit he'd feared for so long.

A previous owner of the house, perhaps? Come to check on his guests?

The flavor began to fade. Within a few minutes, it was gone. The air against Vincent's face warmed, though not markedly so.

Not a strong haunting. Still, Vincent preferred to sleep without ghosts peeking in on him in the middle of the night.

Henry murmured in his sleep, then raised his head. "Vincent? Is something wrong?"

Vincent sat up and reached for his trousers. "I'm not certain," he admitted. At Henry's curious look, he said, "Salt the doors after I've gone back to my room. We've had a visitor."

"A ghost?" Thorpe exclaimed the next morning over breakfast. "In the mansion? Good heavens, I hadn't heard anything about this place being haunted. Though I suppose it hasn't hosted many mediums before, either."

The servants had laid out a hearty spread for their breakfast. Jo tucked in with enthusiasm, but Henry had to force himself to eat. After Vincent revealed they'd had a ghostly visitor, he'd had difficulty returning to sleep, and had woken feeling uncertain and out of sorts.

He ought to be used to it by now, he supposed. Ghosts had the damnable habit of waking him up at night, given the chance. At least he'd slept through the actual manifestation, though according to Vincent it hadn't been a very strong one.

"Are you certain it wasn't just a dream?" Wellington asked, a patronizing smile on his handsome face as he regarded Vincent. "Possibly a bit of dinner, returned on a belch?"

Henry ground his teeth. How dare the fraud accuse Vincent! "Mr. Night has a great deal of experience in these matters," he grated out.

As usual, Vincent's breakfast consisted of coffee and toast. Rather than answer Wellington right away, he measured out some sugar and stirred it into his coffee. "Are you casting aspersions on my ability, Mr. Wellington?" he asked when he was finished. "I was under the impression we're meant to work together."

"Quite right," Thorpe said. "There's no need to get off on a bad foot, Ira."

Lizzie put down her coffee cup. "Mr. Thorpe, I believe you mentioned letters last night?"

Thorpe immediately turned all his attention to answering her. Vincent and Wellington glared at one another across the table. Miss Blake, who had changed into men's clothing for their excursion, raised a brow but said nothing.

Henry took a deep breath and willed himself to calm. Wellington had already cost him too much. He wouldn't let the man cost Vincent and Lizzie their best chance at discovering what their mentor had truly been up to.

"Indeed," Thorpe said. "Alas, none of them are in my actual possession."

A dead end. But perhaps Thorpe could yet enlighten them in some fashion. "Jo had a thought this morning," Henry said. No need to let anyone suspect they'd been meeting in secret. "You said you bought the property at auction. Who owned it previously?"

"That's actually quite interesting," Thorpe said. He tapped the soft-boiled egg sitting in its cup by his plate, then peeled off the shell as he spoke. "The Marsdens, in addition to being the matron and superintendent, were also the owners of the orphanage. Quite an unusual situation, but of course the entire enterprise was the inspiration of Mrs. Marsden and her spirit guide, Xabat. I suppose she didn't wish to answer to anyone else."

"Were they ever declared dead?" Henry asked. "Who were their heirs?"

"I'm uncertain whether they were declared dead—many records were lost when West Virginia separated from Virginia." Thorpe leaned toward Henry. "Mrs. Marsden's son inherited the property. Why he left it to rot, I've no idea. Apparently he—or someone—paid the property taxes on it for decades, up until last year. Attempts were made to locate him, but without result. There was speculation he'd changed his name, or left for Europe, or even died. For whatever reason, no one was able to locate him or any other heirs, and so the property was seized by the state and sold."

Lizzie touched the back of Thorpe's hand with her own. "Mrs. Marsden had a son?"

Thorpe looked down at her hand, for a moment seeming to forget what he was about to say. Then he recovered and offered her a brilliant smile. "Oh yes. From her first marriage, to a Mr. Dunne, though her second husband fully adopted the boy. He and his sister lived at the orphanage with the other children." Thorpe cocked his head in thought. "His name was…give me a moment, and it will come to me…ah yes, I remember. His name was James."

Shocked silence descended around the table. Vincent's copper skin turned a grayish hue, and Lizzie swayed in her chair. Jo gaped like a fish.

Which, considering they were trying to hide their connection with Angel's Shadow, looked damned suspicious. Indeed, a frown had already developed on Wellington's face.

"One moment," Henry said, hoping to draw attention to himself until his companions recovered, "I thought you said everyone from the orphanage vanished. Was the son already grown when the incident happened, or…?"

"Mrs. Marsden's letters indicated he and his sister Arabella were to be raised alongside the other children," Thorpe said.

"…what might our lives have been, if Arabella hadn't betrayed us?" Ortensi had written in his journal.

"His *sister?*" Vincent said faintly. Lizzie's face had gone white.

God. Henry cleared his throat. "So they were alive somewhere?" Henry asked. "The son and daughter?"

"Not that I could discover." Thorpe paused for a sip of his coffee. "However, *someone* continued to pay the taxes on the property in the son's name until recently. As I mentioned, many records were lost during the War Between the States." He glanced from Henry to Lizzie. "I have no reason to think it wasn't the younger Mr. Marsden, of course. But, assuming it was him, we don't know why he left so abruptly and seemingly never returned. Or if he was on the premises when everyone else vanished. I asked around the town, but no one admitted to ever seeing or knowing him, so if he ever returned, he made no show of it."

Vincent took a deep swig from his coffee, but left his toast untouched. "Perhaps the spirits in the orphanage can shed some light on this mystery."

"Indeed." Thorpe beamed at them all. "Let's go ask them, shall we?"

# CHAPTER 6

**VINCENT STARED AT** the passing landscape as the cart made its way from the town, up a winding mountain trail, to the abandoned orphanage. After Thorpe's revelations at breakfast, he'd chosen to ride in the cart hauling Henry's equipment, rather than in Thorpe's carriage.

Henry drove the cart, Vincent beside him, and Jo perched in the back so as to keep an eye on their boxes of equipment. The sun shone down through branches bare of leaves. Enormous trees cut off the mountain vista; the forest appeared to have remained undisturbed for a century. Only the fading ruts of the old road gave any sign humans had ever set foot on this side of Angel Mountain.

Vincent wished Lizzie were in the cart with them. He desperately needed to talk to her. But she'd accepted Thorpe's offer to accompany him in his carriage, along with Miss Blake. Thorpe hadn't wished to bring any servants, so Wellington drove.

Although, really, what was there to say? They'd both been taken in by Dunne, fooled more thoroughly than any mark. Had he ever spoken the truth to them? Or had everything just been an awful lie from beginning to end?

"I take it you had no idea," Henry said, once they were truly into the wilderness.

Vincent glanced at the carriage ahead of them, but of course there was no chance of being overheard. "No." Vincent opened his tin of cinnamon cachous and popped one into his mouth. "Dunne said he'd been raised in an orphanage. Neither of us ever thought to ask if he really was an orphan."

"Why would you? Especially as he never mentioned inheriting the place," Henry said. "Blast. I'm sorry, Vincent. If nothing else, perhaps you and Lizzie could have sold it for a bit of money."

"That's the least of my concerns now, Henry, but thank you."

"What Henry means," Jo said from the back, "is Mr. Dunne should have taken better care of you." Her lips pressed together with displeasure. "He doesn't seem like a very nice man."

"He was, though. Or we thought he was. Which is what makes it all so difficult." Vincent stared blindly down at his hands. "If he'd beaten us, or shown cruelty toward others, perhaps I could accept all this. But he never met a beggar without a coin and a kind word. He never so much as spoke harshly to Lizzie or me, in all the years we were with him." Vincent swallowed the dissolving remnants of the cachou. "I can't reconcile it."

"In his journal, Ortensi said Arabella betrayed them somehow," Henry said. "Prevented them from bringing about paradise, whatever that means."

"Dunne's sister." One more thing Dunne had never breathed a word of.

"We'll find answers at the orphanage," Henry said firmly. "I'm certain of it."

Jo nodded. "Henry's right, Vincent. If nothing else, it seems like the orphanage had something to do with the Grand Harmonium. Why else would Dunne have held onto it all those years?"

"I hope you're right." If not, Vincent didn't know what they would do. "So far, this trip has only raised more questions."

"I wonder why Ortensi didn't try to buy the property," Henry mused. "Or why he didn't alert the authorities as to the fact Dunne had died, but had heirs."

"It slipped his mind?" Vincent hazarded. "Perhaps he didn't realize there were bills to be paid, even after all these years. Dunne was always the one who stayed home and took care of the details, while Ortensi traveled."

"I wish he hadn't fallen off the arc light tower." Henry's features grew troubled at the memory.

Vincent didn't care to recall it either, though for different reasons. The sight of Henry, dangling over the courtyard far below, had seared itself rather unpleasantly into his memory. "It was you or him. Which wasn't a choice at all."

Henry glanced at the carriage in front of them, then put his hand on Vincent's knee, giving it a squeeze. Vincent leaned into him so their shoulders bumped together.

The trees seemed to cluster ever closer to either side of the overgrown track. Dried seed pods rattled on the breeze like the click of bones. Clouds dimmed the sun, and the wind picked up. Angel Mountain towered over them, its green flanks interrupted by swathes of bald gray stone. Soon the road wrapped around the foot of a slope so steep it was nearly a cliff. The looming outcroppings of rock, interrupted by stunted trees clinging to life, lent the view an oppressive air. A stream flowed from a crevice in the cliff, cutting across the road. Fortunately, it was shallow enough to cross with ease.

"What a grim place to build an orphanage," Jo said with a shiver. "Can you imagine growing up here?"

"Perhaps it's more cheerful in the spring," Henry suggested.

Hard to imagine Dunne walking these woods. Riding up this road. He'd been a creature of the city when Vincent met him. Or at least presented himself as such.

The road went around a sharp bend, and Henry caught his breath. "We're there."

A high wall of gray stone appeared through the trees. Black iron spikes slowly rusted atop the wall, sending reddish streaks like bloody tears to stain the rock beneath. The only opening appeared to be an enormous iron gate. ANGEL'S SHADOW ORPHANAGE was spelled out on an arch above, with the stylized image of an eye beneath the iron letters. Vincent recognized it as a symbol of enlightenment.

A new chain and padlock hung across the rusting gates. One gate had come off its lower hinge and sunk partially into the ground. Thorpe descended from the carriage, unlocked the padlock, and hauled open the still-serviceable gate. Someone must have oiled the hinges, as it swung open with a minimal amount of shrieking.

"Dunne doesn't seem to have been interested in maintaining the place," Henry remarked.

"No." Vincent's heart sank. "He and Ortensi were focused on completing the Grand Harmonium. It can't be here. They wouldn't have just let the place fall apart if it were."

"Unless they didn't want to draw attention to it," Jo countered. "If people thought the orphanage was haunted *and* a dangerous wreck, they'd be more likely to stay away. If it seemed well-kept, curiosity alone would surely draw someone inside."

"True," Vincent said as the cart began to move forward again. "Even if the Harmonium itself isn't here, surely we'll find some clue as to where it might be. Or at least what precisely it does differently from ordinary necromancy."

Past the gates, the cliff above them grew more sheer. Its barren gray stone formed the backdrop for the orphanage proper. Rather than placing the building amidst the trees, where light and air might be more easily obtained, the structure backed directly against the natural wall of stone. Even if there were windows in the rear of the three-story structure, they would surely open onto nothing but lichen-encrusted rock.

It seemed a strange choice, to say the least. Mrs. Marsden's spirit guide had directed her to build on this location, according to Thorpe. Had Xabat also guided her as to the strange placement?

The orphanage looked to be wider than it was deep, its walls made of the same gray stone as the cliff, so it almost blended into the mountainside behind it. The windows appeared to be mostly intact, though a clock tower in the center, above the entrance, had collapsed in on itself. Vines crawled up the walls, clinging to crumbling mortar.

An almost breathless air hung around the place. There came no call of birds, or chatter of squirrels, or the other sounds of nature Vincent had become reluctantly acquainted with. The empty windows seemed to glare at them.

If ever an abandoned place wanted to remain abandoned, this one did.

They came to a halt at the base of the short flight of steps leading up to the entryway. Everyone alighted, and Thorpe went to the foot of the stairs. "Today marks a grand occasion," he said, beaming at them as he did so. "The first truly thorough, truly scientific investigation of a haunted property. I shall be taking notes throughout, and cannot wait until our good work here is reported in every psychical journal in this country and abroad."

He seemed sincere. If he did know about the Grand Harmonium, perhaps Lizzie was right, and his interest wasn't purely mercenary.

Vincent found a place beside Miss Blake. She met his gaze, then gave him a little grin and a roll of the eyes. Lizzie, however, seemed raptly focused on Thorpe's words, nodding along with them. Of course, so was Henry. Wellington seemed oddly bored by the speech, stifling a yawn behind his hand and throwing impatient looks at the front door.

Vincent took a deep breath as Thorpe mounted the stairs to the front door and drew out a key. There came the scrape of rusty tumblers, followed by a click. Thorpe threw open the door with a showman's flourish.

"Ladies, gentlemen," he said with a bow to them, "let us begin."

Henry returned to the cart with Jo just long enough to equip themselves with thermometers to measure cold spots and a notebook to record their findings. After their initial survey of the house, they'd choose places to set up the rest of their equipment: Franklin Bells, barometers, and a ghost grounder or two just in case. The Electro-Séance would come out once they'd established the best place to contact whatever spirits still lingered in the orphanage.

God, Henry hoped some spirits lingered here. Moreover, he prayed they were the talkative sorts who would happily share anything they knew about James Dunne—or James Marsden, whatever name they'd known him by—and Ortensi. Not to mention Arabella and the Grand Harmonium.

And if the spirits chose to reveal Wellington as a fraud, so incontrovertibly that Thorpe would have nothing more to do with him, even better.

He and Jo rejoined the rest of the group clustered around the open door. "I suggest we go in one at a time and report our findings," Vincent said. "Just of the front hall. As a little experiment."

He smiled at Wellington as he said it. Wellington smiled back, as if he had not a care in the world. "An excellent suggestion. I shall go first. Mr. Thorpe, Mr. Strauss, neither of you have any mediumistic talents— would you care to accompany me and listen to my impressions first hand?"

The nerve of the fellow. Henry struggled to keep his emotions from his face. "An excellent idea. Jo, I'll need you to record anything we find with our instruments."

Wellington glanced somewhat lower than the thermometer Henry held in his hand. "And such a fine instrument it is."

Vincent's lip curled into a snarl. Thorpe seemed happily oblivious, however, and only said, "Miss Devereaux, Miss Blake?"

"I don't see why not," Miss Blake said with a shrug.

"As my talents are psychometry and automatic writing, I doubt my first impressions will be particularly valuable," Lizzie demurred.

Thorpe entered the building, and Henry followed after, with Jo behind him. Though some light leaked in through the open doorway, the hall stretching out in front of them quickly vanished into impenetrable darkness.

"Why build in such a lightless spot?" Henry murmured. "On the north side of the mountain, right against a cliff, hardly seems a healthful location. Did Mrs. Marsden mention such in the letters you read?"

"Only that her spirit guide instructed her where to build." Thorpe glanced around. "Still, one would think she would have placed the orphanage away from the cliff itself."

Henry knew little of spirit guides, save that they were a favorite trick of frauds. Supposedly they were ghosts of the departed who lingered in order to give information and guidance to the living by possessing mediums. Neither Vincent nor Lizzie had such a guide, nor had their mentor, so Henry hadn't given them much thought.

One would think even the most otherworldly spirit would have recalled enough of life to know such a dank place was hardly suitable for the health of children, though.

Thorpe struck a match and set it to the lantern he'd brought with him. Its illumination drove back the shadows, though not by much. The darkness itself seemed almost to resist the spread of light, enfeebling it.

There was little in the way of a foyer; rather, the doors opened onto a hallway stretching to either side. The gloom seemed to cling to the space directly across from them. Frowning, Thorpe raised his lantern higher.

A pale shape loomed out of the blackness at them.

Henry yelped, and Jo let out a startled squeak. The lantern trembled in Thorpe's hand, causing the shadows to jump. Henry received the impression of a tall figure, standing atop a low plinth, robes draped around it, wings spread...

"It's a statue," he said.

Thorpe blinked...then chuckled ruefully. "So it is, Mr. Strauss. Goodness, but it did give me a turn."

The marble sculpture depicted an angel, presumably the one the orphanage took its name from. It stood in a shallow alcove directly across from the main doors, wings spread protectively and a stern look on its face. One hand reached out toward them, in either supplication or blessing. The other pointed at its feet.

With the scare past, heat crept over Henry's face. "We should take some readings, Jo, before our medium friends come inside," he said in an attempt to conceal his embarrassment.

The air felt colder than outside, although the gloom might account for the difference. Henry consulted the thermometer while Jo recorded their findings.

Thorpe summoned Wellington inside. Henry pretended to ignore him, examining the thermometer instead.

"I like to begin with a small prayer," Wellington said. The damned hypocrite. He took out a small cross of gold, studded with emeralds. Had he used Henry's money to buy it?

Cradling it in his hands, Wellington murmured to it under his breath. Once finished with his prayer, he stepped into the hallway. Henry watched him carefully for any indication of fraud.

"This is an unhappy place," Wellington murmured.

Henry barely kept back a snort. It hardly took a medium to describe a damp, nearly lightless ruin as unhappy.

Wellington closed his eyes, his brows drawing together. "We're being watched." He opened his eyes and stared in the direction of the angel statue. "I sense a male spirit. A man, but young, at the time of his death."

"The teacher? Mr. Everett?" Thorpe suggested.

"Perhaps. He doesn't want us here. He's watching to see what we do." Wellington frowned again. "He sees this as his…station? Like a soldier standing guard."

What a bunch of hogwash. "Standing guard against what?" Henry challenged.

"I'm not certain. Intruders, presumably."

"Excellent," Thorpe said. He scribbled enthusiastically in his notebook. "I imagined it would take some time to locate a spirit, and yet here's one waiting to greet us almost on the very doorstep! Can you send in Miss Blake? Do make certain not to mention your findings to either her or Mr. Night, so we can compare our results."

Miss Blake entered, hands in her pockets and her hat rakishly cocked. The moment she drew abreast of them, however, she stopped. Her eyes fixed on the statue of the angel.

"Huh," she said. "He's a strong apparition for a place deserted for years. Usually the living have to stir things up a bit first."

Henry and Jo exchanged a glance. Could Miss Blake be in on the fraud with Wellington?

"What do you see?" Thorpe asked.

"A man. Youngish, though that doesn't mean anything. A ghost's appearance is more about how it sees itself than how it looked in life.

Dark clothing, so far as I can tell, with smears of chalk dust on it. Ink on his fingers." She shook her head slowly. "He's glaring. Angry. He doesn't want us here."

Blast. If Blake and Wellington were working together, it would be far harder to expose them.

"Where is he?" Jo asked.

Miss Blake pointed to spot just in front of the statue. "Right there."

"Henry, shall we take a temperature reading?"

Of course. At least Jo hadn't let emotion cloud her thinking. "Excellent suggestion, Jo."

Henry strode forward, thermometer held before him like a rapier. "Be careful, Mr. Strauss," Miss Blake called behind him. "He's right—"

Icy cold engulfed Henry's hand, as though he'd thrust his arm into a snowbank. Shock nearly caused him to drop the thermometer. The mercury within its glass tube began to fall rapidly.

"Twenty-eight degrees," Henry gasped, teeth starting to chatter. He snatched his hand back and stepped away from the seemingly empty space.

"He didn't like that," Blake said, taking a step back. "He—"

The lantern flame shifted from yellow to blue, and the temperature around them plunged. A heavy force slammed into Henry's chest, like hands shoving him back. He struck the floor, skidding over the filthy tiles.

"Henry!" Jo shouted, at the same time Thorpe let out a cry of shock.

The light reverted to ordinary yellow. "I think that took all the energy he had to spare, at least for now," Miss Blake said.

Jo knelt by Henry. There came heavy footfalls, and Vincent rushed inside. "Jo? Did I hear you—Henry!"

Henry coughed and struggled to sit up. His chest ached, but at least nothing seemed broken. "It would seem the place is indeed haunted," he managed to say. "And at least one of the ghosts doesn't like guests."

"Or at least ones who poke him with a thermometer," Miss Blake put in.

Vincent put a hand to Henry's elbow, helping him up. "I taste blood," Vincent said uneasily. "Mixed with chalk dust. Fading now."

"We think the ghost was Mr. Everett, the teacher," Thorpe put in. Unease had settled over his handsome face; perhaps he hadn't realized his investigation might be dangerous.

"We all need to carry salt with us," Vincent said, a reproving note in his voice.

Henry winced, knowing it was directed at him. "You're right, and I know better than to not have any with me. I let myself get distracted."

"Understandable." Vincent turned to Thorpe. "Ordinarily spirits need to feed on the energy of the living for a while before becoming strong enough to manifest in such a physical fashion. I'm not certain what's happening here, but we need to be very cautious."

"Yes." Thorpe paused. "I don't wish to put anyone in danger. Perhaps this idea was less brilliant than I originally believed."

Miss Blake let out a chuckle. "Civilians, eh?" she asked, casting a conspiratorial glance at Vincent. "I dare say we've all been knocked about by spirits a time or two. Just have your salt at the ready and you'll be fine. And maybe don't go poking ghosts."

"And be careful on stairs," Henry added. "The push I got didn't hurt me here, but if I'd been at the top of a flight of stairs…"

"I see." Thorpe looked uneasily in the direction of the statue. "Well. Let's go tell the others what happened, and continue our investigation, shall we?"

"Yes. The others," Henry said.

Vincent frowned, but Henry only shook his head. He couldn't say it aloud in front of Thorpe without the risk of giving away all the things they wanted to stay hidden. But it seemed Wellington had told the truth yesterday. Though he'd lied and pretended with Henry and his mother, the man had a real mediumistic gift.

And if he'd been honest about that…what else might he have told the truth about?

# CHAPTER 7

VINCENT WATCHED HENRY out of the corner of his eye. Something had happened to disturb him, beyond the unexpected attack from the spirit. Likely something to do with Wellington. If he had the opportunity, he'd try to get Henry alone and discover what troubled him.

They'd regrouped on the stairs outside. "We should try to find out how the teacher died," Vincent suggested, with a nod toward the now-closed front door.

"If he's angry, he may not be cooperative," Lizzie pointed out. "We should get a sense of the rest of the building and any other spirits within, before we start laying plans."

Vincent swallowed back his own impatience. "You're right, of course."

"I want everyone to be careful," Thorpe said. "One of our number has already been attacked. Hopefully any other spirits within are less violent, but we must all be on our guards. And of course, anyone who wishes to back out now may do so. I certainly wouldn't judge you for it."

"Nonsense," Wellington said. "A small temper tantrum from a spirit surely isn't enough to deter anyone experienced in these matters."

Vincent had been convinced Wellington meant to perpetrate some sort fraud. But venturing into a crumbling building inhabited by at least one hostile spirit seemed a difficult way to go about it. Though Thorpe's offer of payment had been generous, it wasn't extravagant.

Which meant Wellington must be expecting to enrich himself in some other fashion. Say, selling off parts of the Grand Harmonium?

"I suggest each medium and Mr. Strauss visit all the rooms in the orphanage at some point, to give us a complete picture," Thorpe said. "Though all three of the mediums who went inside sensed the spirit, each did so in a unique fashion."

All three? Vincent glanced at Wellington. Did this have something to do with what had upset Henry?

"What can you tell us about the layout of the building?" Miss Blake asked.

"Only generalities. The first floor includes areas such as the dining room, classroom, chapel, among other things." Thorpe gestured vaguely. "The second floor consisted of private quarters for Mr. and Mrs. Marsden, their two children, and most of the staff."

Vincent's heart beat slightly faster. He and Lizzie had to get to Dunne's room first, before anyone else.

"The third floor contained the dormitories for the children and the room for the nurse, Miss Gibson." Thorpe gestured again. Vincent craned his head back and stared at the blank windows high above. Grime filmed them, like cataracts over lidless eyes.

Miss Blake's breath caught audibly. "I saw a face at one of the third-floor windows. Just for a moment."

"One of the children?" Jo asked. "Or an adult?"

She shook her head. "I couldn't tell. But it seems Mr. Everett isn't the only spirit aware of our presence."

"We'll exercise the utmost caution," Lizzie said. "We're already making progress."

Thorpe cocked his head. "In what way?"

"It seems as though the local legends are true, and at least some of the previous inhabitants of the orphanage died." Lizzie paused, then added grimly, "Which raises the question of what became of their bodies, as the original searchers found no trace."

"Could they be in the woods?" Jo asked.

Henry shifted his grip on his thermometer. "But if so, why are the ghosts in here, and not out there?"

"Perhaps we shall learn the answer within," Thorpe said. "To that end, I suggest we return inside and begin our work. Given the reception we've already received from the spirits, I don't want to linger too close to sundown. The mountain will block much of the light, and darkness will come quickly."

At least the man had a sense of caution, unlike some of their previous employers. "Lizzie and I will start with the second floor," Vincent said. Thorpe's lips parted, as though he meant to offer to accompany them, so Vincent quickly added, "Mr. Thorpe, I think you'll find Henry's technique quite unlike anything you've seen at a séance. I recommend you avail yourself of the opportunity to watch him work."

Disappointment flickered in Thorpe's eyes, and Vincent guessed he'd been hoping to be paired with Lizzie. Still, he was too mannerly to contradict Vincent. "Thank you, Mr. Night. If Mr. Strauss has no objections...?"

If Henry wondered what Vincent was about, he didn't let on. "You're quite welcome to observe, Mr. Thorpe. Jo, shall we start on the first floor?"

"And not have to carry any heavy equipment up the stairs? Yes, please."

"Not carry any heavy equipment up the stairs *yet,*" Henry corrected.

"Leaving the third floor for Miss Blake and me," Wellington said, giving her a little bow. She returned the gesture.

Thorpe nodded. "It shall make a good start. There are enough lanterns in the cart for us all. Since it seems at least one ghost is unusually energetic, please be careful, and don't hesitate to call out if you have any need."

"Watch the floors, too," Miss Blake added. "No sense looking out for ghosts if you fall through a rotted hole into the basement." She paused. "Is there a basement?"

"I didn't find mention of one." Thorpe turned to survey the cliff face looming above them. "I wasn't able to locate the original plans for the building, however, only a vague description from the farmer's boy—well, man now—who discovered the place abandoned. Perhaps the stone here proved too intractable."

"That would be a relief," Vincent murmured to Lizzie. Nothing good ever happened in basements, in his experience.

Thorpe surveyed the group. "Any other questions? No? Then let us begin our investigation."

While the mediums made their way up the stairs at one end of the long hall, Henry, Jo, and Thorpe opened some of the crates in the back of the cart.

"Franklin bells," Henry said, digging through the straw packing. Thankfully the instruments had survived the journey from Baltimore intact. "Barometer to measure atmospheric pressure."

"What about the ghost grounder?" Jo asked, holding up a length of copper rod.

It would have been useful against Everett. Henry's chest still ached where the ghost had struck him. Unfortunately, the grounder wasn't the most portable piece of equipment, as it had to be connect to some sort of grounding rod via copper wire. "Not yet. We'll arm ourselves with salt for now."

Thorpe shook his head admiringly. "You are indeed prepared for almost anything, it would seem. What's in the other crates?"

"Pieces of the Electro-Séance. The phantom fence, the dispeller, a Wimshurst machine to generate electro-magnetic energy for the ghosts to feed on. An arc light."

"And the arc headlamps," Jo added. "In case it turns out there is a basement after all."

"Perish the thought," Henry said fervently. They'd removed a rather nasty spirit lurking in the dark corner of a basement only last month. The headlamp had come in rather handy, though, enough to make the fashioning of a second a priority. "The rest of our equipment consists mainly of batteries and more salt."

They proceeded into the hallway, leaving the doorway standing wide. The thought of the teacher's spirit returning and coming up behind them unnoticed left Henry uneasy, so he said, "Let's put a line of salt across the entry to the recess. If Everett returns, hopefully he'll be trapped near the statue."

"Mr. Wellington did say he was like a man standing guard," Thorpe said. "Do you think Everett sees this as his post in some fashion?"

Henry didn't want to think about anything Wellington had said. Even less about the fact he apparently had actual gifts, and had simply chosen not to use them in his twisted revenge on Henry's family. "Hard to say," Henry said neutrally. "Jo, if you'd hand me the bag?"

Henry's skin prickled as he laid down the salt. But there was no sense of being watched as there had been before. Apparently, the spirit had indeed expended all its strength in its attack on Henry.

For the moment, anyway. But the longer they were in the building, the more active the haunting would become. Their own energy would feed the ghost, whether they wished it to or not.

Once the salt was in place, Henry led the way down the left-hand portion of the main hall and toward the stairs the others had taken to the upper floors. The occasional creak and groan filtered down from above, which Henry assumed to be the result of the mediums moving around, rather than a sign of ghostly activity.

Immediately to the left was a door marked OFFICE in tarnished brass letters. Henry opened the door cautiously and entered first, one hand on his thermometer, the other hovering near the small bag of salt in his pocket.

Little light filtered through the dirt covered window. Black mold streaked the outer wall, perhaps indicating a leaky roof far above. An old desk dominated the room, along with a broken chair. A wooden cabinet stood against one wall, its fittings gone green with tarnish. The air stank of mildew and damp wood.

"Do you think there might be any records in there?" Jo asked, pointing to the cabinet.

"It's worth a look." Thorpe tugged on the latch and was rewarded with a shriek of unoiled hinges.

Several leather-bound journals—or perhaps ledgers—filled one shelf. Mildew spotted them, and when Thorpe took one out, the pages proved to be badly warped by moisture. Still, Henry's heart leapt at the sight of legible writing. Perhaps there would be something in the journals to help Lizzie and Vincent.

"I'll check these," Thorpe said. "Why don't the two of you investigate the desk?"

Decades of neglect had warped the once-fine wood. He and Jo wrestled open first one drawer, then another, each screaming in protest. Any papers inside were nothing more than piles of mold. As Jo waved a hand in front of her face, Henry glanced back over his shoulder at Thorpe, intending to report their lack of findings.

But the words died on his tongue when Thorpe slipped a ledger from the cabinet into his coat.

Vincent had suspected Thorpe of hiding something from them. It seemed he'd been right. Logic suggested it had some connection to the Grand Harmonium, as there seemed little else about this rotted heap worth taking.

Blast.

"Nothing here," Henry said.

Thorpe started. "Nor here," he said, hastily shutting the cabinet. "Merely accounting lists—how many pounds of salted ham ordered for the week, that sort of thing."

Henry was willing to bet the ledger Thorpe had taken wasn't a mere account book. "A shame."

"Shall we continue on?" Thorpe asked, already moving to the door.

Across from the office lay a small chapel. It had no windows, and its back wall had been left unfinished, the raw rock of the mountain exposed behind the rotting remains of the altar. The gray stone came unexpectedly alive in the light of their lanterns, thousands of fragments of blue crystal glinting like tiny stars.

"How lovely," Thorpe said. "During services, with a few dozen candles burning, it must have been quite a beautiful effect. I'm starting to see why they chose to put the chapel here, at least."

A breeze touched Henry's face. "Does anyone else feel the air moving?"

"A spirit?" Thorpe asked in alarm.

Henry pulled out his bag of salt. But Jo crouched by the altar. "I don't think so. Look—there's a crack in the floor."

Indeed, the marble tiles had split not far from the wall. Henry knelt by the fissure. A cool breeze blew up through it. "Perhaps there is a basement after all," he murmured. Reaching into his satchel, he pulled out a box of matches and struck one. He held it to the crack, but only darkness lay below. On impulse, he let go of the match. The spark fell, much farther than he'd expected, before going out.

"Be careful," he said, motioning for Jo to move back. "The floor here might not be as solid as it looks. There appears to be an open space beneath us."

"A basement?" Thorpe suggested.

"Heaven forbid." Henry got to his feet. "All sorts of nasty things tend to lurk in basements."

Jo still crouched beside the altar, despite his admonishment to move away. "Henry, look," she said, pointing to the floor near her feet.

Someone had set a large, brass plaque into the tiles. Time had left it badly tarnished, but the cast letters were still legible.

IN MEMORIAM
BETSY MARSDEN
MELVILLE MARSDEN
WILLIAM EVERETT
MARY GIBSON
QUINCY BROWN
RAMON GREEN
FAITH MOREHOUSE
PEARL SMITH

MURDERED JULY 12, 1849 BY A.D.M.

"DEATH IS BUT SLEEP."

"Murdered," Thorpe whispered. "My God."

Henry reached out and ran a trembling hand over the initials. A. D. M.

Arabella Dunne Marsden?

A loud crash sounded from the other side of the wall.

"I'm sorry to have had to put off Mr. Thorpe," Vincent said as he and Lizzie emerged onto the second floor. "But with any luck, Dunne's old quarters will be here, with the…rest of the family." The sickening sense of betrayal rolled through him again.

Lizzie's lips were a tight, white line behind her thin veil. "Everything was a lie, Vincent. Everything. A mother. A *sister*."

"Arabella. Ortensi wrote she'd betrayed them, somehow."

"Dunne never mentioned any of it. Not once." She shook her head. "We never knew him at all, did we?"

He caught her gloved hand and gave it a squeeze. "It seems as though Arabella's betrayal was grave, if Ortensi was still angry over it all these years later. Perhaps it brought back too many bad memories. Maybe Dunne simply couldn't bring himself to tell us."

"Let's just see if we can find anything." She freed her hand from his and turned her attention to the hallway before them.

Vincent nodded. "Which way?"

The hall they stood in ran from one end of the building to the other, echoing the configuration downstairs. "We might as well start here," Lizzie said, gesturing to the nearest door, which lay to their left.

Vincent opened the door cautiously. No foreign flavors intruded into his mouth like an unwelcome kiss. "I don't sense any spirits yet," he said, stepping inside.

Light filtered through the dirty windows, revealing what had once been a comfortable sitting room. Chairs stood near the fireplace, their cushions long reduced to nests for mice. A writing desk sat beneath the window, and decanters of liquor—long evaporated—lined a sideboard. An inner door opened onto a bedroom, its furnishings similar in style to those of the sitting room.

Lizzie swung open the wardrobe to reveal decayed rags inside.

"From what's left, my guess is this room belonged to Mr. Marsden."

"So it would seem." Vincent ran his tongue along his teeth. "I don't sense any spirits here. Perhaps he moved on."

"Let's hope so."

Lizzie led the way back to the hall. There came a creak from the far end, as though an unseen foot had stepped on a loose floorboard.

"Vincent?" she asked softly.

"I don't sense anything yet. Though if the spirit isn't strong, at this distance..." he trailed off.

"Or the sound may have had a natural cause." Her skirts rustled softly as she started off again. "Come on."

Past Marsden's rooms, the space opened up to the left, into what appeared to have been used as a common parlor. The only light other than their lanterns came from a window set in the front wall of the building, above the lower entryway. Two doors opened off of it.

"Left or right?" Vincent asked.

"Right," Lizzie said.

The door let onto a small, private dining room. What had once been a beautifully carved walnut table now stood filthy and warped from years of neglect. The china cabinet was in equal disrepair, although when Vincent cautiously rubbed some of the grime away with a handkerchief, it revealed intact plates and saucers within.

"No ghosts here either," he said. "Do you think this suite belonged to Mrs. Marsden?"

"Probably. Which means we need to look elsewhere."

They exited and went to the door directly across the common parlor. The room inside proved to be a single chamber, with bed, writing table, wardrobe, and bookshelves. Lizzie opened the wardrobe. "A man's clothing."

"It could belong to the teacher."

"But it's closest to the Marsdens'. Surely the family would be nearest each other."

As they searched the room for some clue to its owner, Vincent half expected flavor to flood his mouth. Surely, if they'd found no trace of Dunne elsewhere, he would have returned here. To his childhood home.

The writing desk yielded up nothing of interest—no letters or even a journal, just what appeared to be completed schoolwork consisting of arithmetic. The books on the shelf consisted of Swedenborg's *The Heavenly Doctrine*, *The Book of Wonders* by Joanna Southcott, and a handful of early spiritualist pamphlets. Lizzie took one of them from the end of the shelf; a combination of damp and mildew caused it to stick unpleasantly to the book beside it. Making a face of distaste, she nevertheless peeled open the cover.

On the frontispiece, a familiar hand had written: *James D. Marsden.*

The taste of sweet taffy filled Vincent's mouth an instant before the door to the room slammed shut.

# CHAPTER 8

"**THE SOUND CAME** from the next room," Jo said.

Henry's pulse kicked in his throat, but he forced his voice to remain steady. "Keep your salt ready, Jo. Mr. Thorpe, allow me to go first."

Double doors led into the next room, and the tarnished plaque on the wall read DINING HALL. Henry poured a handful of salt out of the bag and into his palm, and shoved the doors open.

They swung slowly on their rusted hinges, squealing like dying sows as they did so. The scent of mold and rot billowed out in a cloud, and Henry raised an arm to cover his nose and mouth. Nothing else rushed at them, however, so he took a cautious step inside.

As with the chapel, this room had no windows, and the rough rock of the mountain formed the back wall. The remains of long tables and benches filled most of the room, the wood reduced to slimy fragments. Mushrooms sprouted from the table on a slightly raised dais; unlike the others, this one had individual chairs rather than benches. No doubt the adults had taken their meals there. The chair in the center was larger than the rest, its intricate carvings making it seem more like a throne.

Had Mrs. Marsden sat there? What of her children—had they been favored, or placed among the orphans?

Her children. Had he correctly interpreted the plaque? Had Arabella in fact murdered her own mother and step-father, not to mention the other names on the list?

Dunne must have been the one to place the memorial. His own sister...was this why he'd kept his past secret from Vincent and Lizzie? Did it have less to do with deception and more with grief?

And what about Arabella herself? What had become of her?

"This must have been a gloomy place to dine," Thorpe murmured. "The poor children. How much light did they see in a day? Or were they kept always in darkness?"

A giggle sounded from one corner of the room.

Thorpe gasped, and Jo seized Henry's arm. Henry wished one of the mediums had accompanied them. Lowering the lantern, he stepped toward the corner. "Hello?" he said, voice trembling only slightly. "Who's there?"

The only response was the sound of feet pattering over the floor, as though an unseen child raced straight at them. Before Henry could back away, a wave of cold struck him.

It was like being thrust into a snowbank. The lantern flames turned blue, then went out, plunging them into darkness. Thorpe swore and Jo let out a little squeak, but Henry's tongue was too cold, his lips frozen together. Pain burst in his chest, and for a wild moment he wondered if his heart had stopped.

Then it was gone. There came another giggle, this time from the direction of the hall, footsteps receding into silence.

Henry's knees gave out. He hit the floor with a thump, salt scattering around him as he clutched his chest.

Thorpe struck a match. At the sight of Henry on his knees, Jo hastily crouched by him. "Henry!" She touched his hand with her brown fingers —then snatched them back. "You're like ice!"

Warmth crept back into his blood, though slowly. Thorpe used the match to relight the lantern, which once again burned a cheerful yellow. "I'm all right," he managed to say.

"What happened?" Thorpe asked. "Did it attack you?"

"No. I mean, I don't think so." With Jo's assistance, Henry managed to climb back to his feet. "I think it was meant as nothing more than a childish prank. An unpleasant one for me, but the laughter didn't seem malicious."

Thorpe shifted uneasily. "Is it safe to continue to explore on our own, without a medium?"

Henry hesitated. He'd only just wished a medium was with them, but Vincent and Lizzie needed time to search for any clues Dunne might have left behind. They couldn't do so with Thorpe peering over their shoulders. Henry and Jo needed to keep the man occupied for as long as possible.

Still, it couldn't be denied he'd feel safer with them. The ghosts were damnably active, for a location left abandoned for so long. Ghosts required energy to manifest. Some of it came from the ambient surroundings—drawing heat from the air, for example, which led to cold spots. But ghosts also drew from the energy of the living. Abandoned locations tended to be quiet, their activity slowly increasing over time once the living returned.

Angel's Shadow was far too active for a place so clearly deserted. Unless the ghosts had some other source of energy, which kept them strong even when there were no living humans to feed on.

"You said Mrs. Marsden's spirit guide chose this place," Henry said, an idea forming. "I wonder if it has some special properties. Something keeping the spirits active."

Thorpe frowned. "Such as?"

Henry gestured to the rock wall. "The geomagnetic properties of the stone from which the mountain is formed might have some effect? I should get the galvanometer from the cart and take some measurements."

"Not in here, though," Jo said with a shiver. "I don't like this room. It feels…wrong."

"We still need to explore the classroom, on the other side of the building," Henry said. "Later, we'll fetch the galvanometer and take measurements there, or in the chapel." Hopefully that would give Vincent and Lizzie enough time to conduct their search of the second floor without interference.

Thorpe still seemed uncertain. But he nodded. "Very well, Mr. Strauss. You are the expert in these matters after all. Lead on."

"Vincent!" Lizzie exclaimed.

They both rushed to the door. Footsteps sounded in the hall outside, their tread light.

"Did you hear that?" Lizzie asked. "It sounded like a child laughing."

Thankfully, the door opened easily when Vincent tugged on it. "I tasted taffy," he said. "I think you're right. There is a child's ghost here with us."

"Do you want to attempt contact?" Lizzie asked.

Vincent hesitated. Entering a trance back in Baltimore, in the safe confines of their shop, was one thing. Trying it in the middle of a haunted orphanage, not knowing what might answer his call, was another.

He hadn't always been so cautious. Until the night the malevolent spirit had used his body to murder Dunne.

Vincent swallowed against the sudden dryness in his throat. "Not yet. Let's keep looking. Dunne's room didn't offer any answers, but perhaps Arabella's will be different."

No sooner had they passed through the common parlor and back into the hall, than all the doors they'd opened slammed shut at once with a terrific boom. Vincent and Lizzie both started.

"I don't think they like having the doors open," Vincent murmured.

"Or the child is playing a prank." Lizzie glanced at him. "Do you remember the ghost we exorcized near the Bowery?"

"I hadn't thought of her in years." It had been one of their last trials before Dunne declared their apprenticeship over. The spirit belonged to a young girl who had been scalded to death in a horrible accident. When a new family moved into the tenement apartment where she'd died, she'd wanted to play with the children. Moving their toys about, pinching them, hiding things: frightening but not out of bounds for what a living child might do. Unfortunately, at some point she'd decided it would be more fun if her new playmates were spirits as well. The incidents escalated, becoming very violent very fast.

They'd managed to exorcise her, though not without some terrifying moments, including Lizzie being held pinned on the ceiling and Vincent having boiling water flung at him. All accompanied by the giggling laugh of a young girl. As though it were merely a game to her.

Dunne had been so proud when they walked out the next morning, alive and victorious.

"We survived." All the lightness of the moment, of the pride in pleasing his mentor, turned sour. "Ortensi said other apprentices didn't. She was a test, wasn't she? That was why Dunne let us face her without him."

A tired sigh escaped Lizzie. "Probably. Come on—we need to find Arabella's room before anyone comes looking for us."

The last two rooms clearly belonged to a man—presumably Everett —and a woman who had to be Arabella. But their contents were even more ruined than those of the other chambers. Black mold crawled over every surface, and any papers or books had been reduced to mildewed lumps.

"Drat," Lizzie muttered as they stood in Arabella's room. "I'd hoped for more. For…something."

"Agreed." Turning away from the ruined bookshelves, Vincent tugged on one of the wardrobe doors.

It swung open with a scream of hinges. The clothes that had once hung within were nothing more than rotted tatters heaped on the bottom.

When the wardrobe had been functional, they would have concealed the plain oak panels forming the rear of the compartment. Now, Vincent could clearly see someone had gouged crude letters into the wood.

*Xabat is watching.*
*I can feel its eyes on me, all the time.*
*He will show us the way. Bring the dead back to life.*
*But*
*I*
*Am*
*Afraid*

Just as with the dining hall, the classroom was built against the side of the mountain, without a single window to let in light.

"I don't understand," Henry said, turning in a slow circle, his lantern upheld. "They'd need to spend a fortune on candles and oil, just so the students could see the blackboard. Why on earth not put the classroom at the front of building where the windows are?"

Rows of benches, most of them overturned, filled much of the large room. The accoutrements of education lay scattered about: a globe, its continents obscured by mold; a shelf full of books fused together by rot; individual writing slates heaped in a corner. A large chalkboard hung on the right-hand wall, broken sticks of chalk scattered on the floor all around. As with the other rooms at the back of the building, its rear wall consisted only of the rough, cracked stone of the mountain.

Thorpe's face had gone pale in the dim light. "Were they keeping the children in the dark? Away from light and air? But why would anyone be so cruel?"

Dunne's mother had been behind the design of this place. Vincent and Lizzie both insisted Dunne had no cruelty in him; perhaps he'd suffered too much as a youth. "I wonder if Mrs. Marsden thought it would bring out their mediumistic gifts?" He walked to the wall and put a hand to the stone. Cool, but not cold. Flecks of the strange blue mineral glittered in the lantern light, seeming almost to glow with some inner fire. "If I'm correct and the rock has some unusual geomagnetic properties, perhaps she hoped exposure to them would help...I don't know, open the children even more to the spirits?"

"We've nothing but conjecture," Thorpe said, and the note of disappointment in his voice caused Henry to turn to him.

"We've barely begun our investigation," he said. "And the others may have found something."

"True." Thorpe managed a smile. "We'll—"

"Henry," Jo said in alarm. She stared at the thermometer in her hand. "Look."

Her breath plumed into steam on the last word, the air going from cool to freezing in an instant. Had the child ghost returned? Or was it some new manifestation? If only Vincent were here.

There came a dry, scraping sound from the direction of the chalkboard. Henry turned slowly, the hair on his arms and neck prickling.

A lone piece of chalk hung suspended in air. With agonizing slowness, it squeaked across the slate surface, laboriously writing.

"Oh my God," Thorpe whispered.

The chalk fell to the ground, shattering into powder. Within seconds, the air began to warm again.

Even though the ghost seemed gone, Henry hesitated to approach the chalkboard. But the letters were too small to make out from across the room. Swallowing hard, he forced his knees to unlock and went to the chalkboard. Jo and Thorpe followed on his heels.

Henry stopped the moment he could make out the words. "Jo, don't..."

But it was too late, of course. She let out a gasp and grabbed Henry's arm. "Henry," she said in a shaking voice. "Look at what it wrote."

He slipped a protective arm around her shoulders. Scrawled in a shaky hand, as if the ghost had struggled to hold the chalk, was:

*not safe get out its watching jo im sorry*

Vincent and Lizzie stared at the writing in the wardrobe. Vincent swallowed heavily. "This...doesn't look good."

"Clearly Arabella was under some mental strain," Lizzie murmured. "But look. It says Xabat would show them the way to return the dead to life. Do you think she was referring to the Grand Harmonium?"

Before Vincent could answer, a scream rang out from the floor above. He and Lizzie exchanged a startled glance—then he sprinted for the stairs.

As he emerged into the third story hall, the taste of mint and horehound flooded his mouth. At the same time, a sensation of dread swept over him, accompanied by a freezing wall of air.

Miss Blake crouched in the center of the hall, her arms over her head. Wellington hunkered beside her, his hands clasped around an emerald-studded cross, his lips pressed to it as he murmured unintelligibly. A heavy steel basin lay beside them, a dent in the wall above attesting to the force with which it had been hurled.

"Where is it?" Vincent shouted at Miss Blake, even as he ripped the pouch of salt from inside his coat.

She cringed but pointed at the open door in the center of the hall, only feet from them. Vincent poured out a generous handful of salt and flung it into the space.

Almost instantly, the cold began to fade, along with the mint coating his mouth. "She's retreating into her room!" Miss Blake called encouragingly. "Keep at it!"

Vincent scattered salt in a wide arc. The cold lessened again—then the door slammed shut of its own accord.

Before it could open again, Vincent hastily poured out a line of salt in front of the doorway. "There. Hopefully this will keep it contained."

"It was the nurse," Miss Blake said shakily. Vincent held out his hand and helped her to her feet. Wellington also stood, silent and pale. Vincent couldn't help but feel a vindictive gladness at the sight.

"The nurse?" asked Lizzie. Slowed by her skirts, it had taken her longer to arrive.

Miss Blake nodded. "She looked…terrible. Her face twisted. Her teeth were like needles, and her nails were scalpels." Miss Blake trailed off with a shudder.

"I'm sensing a great deal of anger," Wellington said. "Her rage is born of protectiveness. She's afraid we'll do harm to…something." He tipped his head, confused. "But not the children under her care. Something else."

Vincent gasped, though not because of some insight on Wellington's part. Rather, the last of the nurse's medicinal taste washed from his tongue, replaced instead with cigars and steak.

"The ghost from the mansion," he said, taking a step back. "It's here."

Miss Blake's eyes went wide, and she cast about. "It must not be very strong. Wait, is that...no, it's gone." She shook her head. "I've seen at least one child ghost who manifests only as a shadow, caught from the corner of my eye. It might have been them."

The flavor in Vincent's mouth faded, leaving behind nothing but the lingering cinnamon of his cachous. "Lizzie and I encountered the ghost of a child as well. But this...I'm certain it was the spirit from the mansion."

"The ghost from the mansion?" Wellington demanded skeptically. "Surely not. The buildings are miles apart."

Lizzie's frown showed through the thin material of her veil. "Spirits sometimes attach themselves to a person," she said. "Not frequently, but it does happen."

"But why would it attach itself to me?" Vincent asked. "That doesn't..."

He trailed off. Because there was one possibility which did make sense.

Dunne had enjoyed the occasional cigar. Could he have reached out somehow last night, across the miles, and found Vincent sleeping in Henry's room?

"What have you discovered up here?" Lizzie asked Miss Blake. "Other than an angry nurse, of course."

"The dormitories for the children." Miss Blake pointed to a door they'd run past. "Or one of them, anyway. For the girls, judging by the dolls remaining. I suspect the boys' is on the opposite end of the hall." She hesitated. "The one we looked into didn't have any windows, and the rear wall was just the cliff face. It must have been terribly dark."

"We found another room that might be of interest," Wellington added. Casting a wary look at the salted door, he led the way past the nurse's room.

Like the dormitories, the chamber occupied the rear of the building. A small chalkboard hung on one wall, and half-rotten chairs littered the floor. It might have been a classroom, save for the other items scattered about.

"Instruments," Vincent said, picking up a tarnished harmonica. "Tables. Cards."

Lizzie put a hand to a wooden cabinet, large enough to seat an adult, its doors standing open. "A spirit cabinet. They used this room to test the psychical abilities of the orphans."

And probably Dunne and Arabella's as well. "You're right." Vincent took a deep breath, tilting his head back. "I don't sense anything."

"I think the children hid themselves when the nurse came out," Miss Blake offered. "At least, I'm not seeing shadows peeking around the corners anymore."

There came the faint sound of a voice. They all froze, listening intently.

"Miss Devereaux?" it called from the direction of the stairs. "Are you up there?"

"That's Mr. Thorpe." Lizzie hurried out of the room. "We're here!" she called. "Wait and we'll come to you."

Wellington and Miss Blake followed her, clearly having seen everything they felt they needed to see. Vincent took a final look over the room.

Dunne had been in the hall with them, he was certain of it. Protecting them from the nurse, or trying to do so.

He'd visited the mansion once before. If they could find something of his to strengthen the connection...

There. In the corner of the room lay a student's slate with a broken frame. Though the beginning of the student's name was obscured by the damage, the letters D. MARSDEN were still visible.

D. Marsden. James Dunne Marsden.

"Vincent?" Lizzie called from the hall.

He snatched up the slate and tucked it inside his coat. "Coming!" he shouted, and went to join her, the slate knocking against his chest with every step like the beating of a second heart.

# CHAPTER 9

"IT KNEW MY name," Jo said with a shiver. "How did it know my name?"

The slight quiver in her voice sent a pang through Henry's chest. She had faced ghosts alongside them before, but Henry had never imagined he might not be able to protect her. Though of course he'd thought any harm would be physical, not this...intimidation or whatever it was.

"A good question," he said, handing her a cup of hot tea. "Does anyone have an answer?"

They'd regrouped outside at the cart, all with their own tales of encountering ghosts. Some of the spirits, like the children, seemed harmless. But the adults at least seemed angry at their intrusion. They'd returned to the mansion under a cloudy sky and a cold wind. A roaring fire in the study, accompanied by hot tea, proved a welcome relief. Everyone else arranged themselves around the room, helping themselves to tea or, in Miss Blake's case, a stiff brandy.

"Mrs. Marsden only took orphans with mediumistic talents," she said, sipping at the brandy. "Perhaps they have psychical ability beyond what one would encounter in ordinary ghosts."

"Perhaps." Vincent sat on Jo's other side. "Nothing about Angel's Shadow feels ordinary."

"Agreed," said Lizzie. She perched on the same chair she'd occupied the night before, Thorpe once again at her side. "I've never seen a haunting like this."

Thorpe turned to Henry. "You mentioned the stone might have unusual properties?"

"Do enlighten the rest of us, Henry," Lizzie said with the arch of a brow.

Henry flushed slightly as every eye turned to him. "It's but a theory. Mrs. Marsden's spirit guide directed her where to build. Rather than place the orphanage away from the cliff face, it was built directly against the mountainside, the rear wall unfinished so the raw stone was exposed."

Thorpe took a gulp of his tea, as if drawing strength from it. "All the rooms with no windows, with only lantern light and the reflections of the crystals within the stone, were those the children would have regularly occupied. The dining hall, the classroom, the dormitories."

"The training room for their mediumistic talents," Vincent added. He met Henry's gaze over the top of Jo's head. "Do you think Mrs. Marsden was trying to…I don't know, influence their development by exposing them to whatever properties the stone has?"

"I couldn't say. Nor could I guess whether it would affect the living." Henry took a sip of his own tea and winced at its bitterness. He'd forgotten to add any sugar. "If it does contain strong geomagnetic properties, though, it could provide the ghosts a constant energy source from which to draw."

"Interesting theory, Henry," Wellington said. "You might be onto something."

Henry didn't like the speculative look in his eye, nor the familiarity of Wellington's tone. "I could be incorrect. Perhaps for the moment we should concentrate on facts."

"Very well," Lizzie said. "Here are our facts. Henry, Jo, and Mr. Thorpe discovered a plaque in the chapel seeming to indicate Arabella somehow murdered almost every inhabitant of the orphanage. Poison in their food would seem the easiest way for her to have achieved that, but I wouldn't want to jump to conclusions."

"The hidden writing in the back of her wardrobe certainly seemed to indicate a disturbed mind," Vincent added.

Henry frowned. He'd been so concerned for Jo, he hadn't given any thought to the writing in Arabella's room. "You said she'd written something about Xabat watching? And the ghostly writing on the chalkboard said 'it's watching.' Do you think the spirit in the classroom might have been Arabella?"

"It seems possible," Vincent agreed.

Jo shivered. "But how would she know my name? And she murdered a bunch of people…"

Vincent patted her shoulder. "We won't let anything hurt you, Jo."

"I know." She made a face. "It just makes my skin crawl."

"So what does the message mean?" Henry asked. Had some spirit been listening in to their conversations, in order to learn her name? Or worse, seeing into their thoughts as Miss Blake had suggested? "If Jo is in some sort of danger…"

He trailed off. Though he'd never imagined himself raising a child, even for a few years, Jo's appearance on his doorstep at age fourteen had proved a blessing in disguise. If only the family hadn't ostracized his uncle for marrying a black woman.

He should have made the effort to reach out, after his mother died and he was left alone and virtually penniless. He'd been so absorbed in his own troubles, he hadn't even spared his uncle's family a thought at the time.

"The meaning of the message would be clearer if the ghost had bothered to use proper punctuation," Lizzie said with a twist of her lips.

Wellington shook his head. "I wouldn't put too much stock in it. The writing was probably done by one of the ghost children as a prank."

Lizzie leveled a frosty glare at him. "May I remind you automatic writing is one of my talents, sir."

"Really, Wellington, I don't know what's gotten into you. We're all on the same side here," Thorpe said. "Go on, Miss Devereaux."

She gave him a small nod. "As I was saying, it would be helpful to know which part of the message was addressed to Jo. *It's watching Jo* or *Jo, I'm sorry?*"

"I don't like the first option, that's for sure," Jo said with a shudder. "Arabella thought the spirit guide was watching her. I don't want it watching me, too."

Miss Blake finished off her brandy. "I wouldn't be too concerned about that, Miss Strauss. Spirit guides do watch over those in their care, but in a protective fashion. No doubt Xabat was indeed concerned about Arabella, if she was mentally unstable."

"I'd say that part is clear enough, as she murdered her own parents," Lizzie said grimly.

"Perhaps it would be for the best if Miss Strauss remains at the mansion?" Thorpe suggested, glancing from Lizzie to Jo. "I would hate to think the ghost of a murderess has taken an interest in her."

Jo's eyes widened, and she turned to Henry. "No! Henry, please, I want to help. You need me."

Henry's first instinct was to agree with Thorpe. "I don't want to expose you to any danger, Jo. The ordinary activity of spirits is worrisome enough, without adding an insane murderess to the mix."

"We don't know Arabella wrote those words," Jo countered. "And even if she did, they sound like a warning, not a threat."

Henry sighed. He didn't want to deny her, but her safety had to be paramount. "We'll discuss it in the morning," he temporized.

"I've got another question," Miss Blake said. She paused to pour a second brandy before continuing. "Someone put that plaque in the chapel, and it must have been after the place was originally searched. Who?"

Henry very carefully didn't glance at either Vincent or Lizzie. Oddly enough, Thorpe coughed and suddenly found something very interesting about the flames in the fireplace.

"The son's name wasn't on the plaque," Wellington said. "Surely it was him."

"What happened to the bodies?" Lizzie asked quickly. "Were they taken away? Interred?"

A chill went through Henry. "We found an unstable bit of floor in the chapel. The tiles were cracked, and it appeared as though there was a space beneath. It might have simply been a collapse under the foundations, if there was a natural cave or hollow place within the mountain. But what if there's a basement?"

"The Marsdens were certainly obsessed with exposure to the stone," Vincent said slowly. "It would make sense for there to be a lower level, hewn out of the mountain itself if need be. But if so, where is the entrance? We searched the building thoroughly."

"An outside entrance?" Jo suggested.

"Dear heavens, I hope not." Vincent made a face. "Traipsing about on the mountainside, or in the woods…"

"It could take months to find," Miss Blake finished. "A shame none of the locals will work with us. We could have them out there, beating the bushes for us."

Silence fell over their little group for a few moments. Then Thorpe stirred. "Perhaps we'll find something more obvious tomorrow," he said. "For now, let's adjourn and spend the evening resting."

"Anyone fancy a game of poker?" Miss Blake asked.

Wellington nodded. "I'll join you."

Henry bit his tongue to keep from warning her to watch for

cheating. He needed to get Vincent, Jo, and Lizzie alone and tell them about the ledger Thorpe had taken. At least the card game would keep Miss Blake and Wellington occupied for a time.

Thorpe rose to his feet. "I thought I'd take a turn around the garden." His handsome face flushed a dark red. "Miss Devereaux, would you, er, care to accompany me?"

A similar flush spread over Lizzie's cheeks. "That would be lovely, Mr. Thorpe."

Well then.

Everyone else drifted out, leaving Vincent, Jo, and Henry alone. As soon as he was certain they wouldn't be overheard, he said, "There's something I need to tell you."

"I knew it," Vincent said, when Henry finished. "Thorpe is hiding something. Perhaps even something relating to the Grand Harmonium." He paused, clearly pondering. "You said he put the ledger inside his overcoat? I can't imagine he's carrying it around while strolling the garden with Lizzie. Too much danger of her feeling it should they find themselves in closer proximity."

Should he worry about Lizzie? But Vincent seemed unconcerned, and surely Lizzie knew how to conduct her own affairs. "No doubt he left it in his room."

"How very convenient he is otherwise occupied."

Jo's eyes widened. "You mean to search Mr. Thorpe's room?"

Vincent's grin showed his teeth. "I do."

Jo stood guard near the stairs, while Henry and Vincent made their way to Thorpe's room. When they reached the door, Henry glanced back and forth. "If we're caught…"

Vincent had the same fears, but he didn't see what else they might do. If they were found out, Thorpe would fire them on the spot and forbid them to return to the orphanage. They might wait for a time, come back after he and the other two mediums left, but who was to say if anything would remain to find? If Thorpe was seeking the Grand Harmonium, he would either take it, if it was in the orphanage, or have a head start on finding it if it was elsewhere.

And then what? Use it for necromancy? Sell it to someone unscrupulous, as Ortensi had feared?

Vincent had sworn to protect both the living and the dead. He couldn't turn his back on that.

"I know." Vincent put a hand briefly to Henry's shoulder. "But it's the only way. Thorpe is hiding something from us, something which might make everything clear. Answer our questions."

"Lizzie will kill us both if she realizes we used her as a distraction."

Vincent winced. Henry wasn't wrong. It was impossible to miss how Lizzie looked at Thorpe—and how he looked at her. Whether there was any hope of things going farther...

Vincent squashed down the urge to play the role of overprotective brother. Lizzie knew her business and wouldn't appreciate his interference.

"Then let's not get caught," he said, and reached for the door latch.

It was unlocked. "Is Thorpe a trusting sort, or does he have nothing to hide, and we're simply being paranoid?" Vincent murmured.

Henry squared his shoulders. "Only one way to find out," he said, and stepped inside.

The master suite was large and well-appointed. A sitting room greeted them, its fire burning low. Henry shut the door behind them, and they both stood in silence for a moment while their eyes adjusted to the dim light coming from the flickering flames.

"Where should we search?" Henry asked. "Do you think he'd leave the ledger out, where the maids would likely find it?"

"A ledger wouldn't look suspicious to the maids," Vincent replied, careful to keep his voice low in case anyone passed by in the hall outside. "Nor would, say, letters or notes. We're looking for anything that might enlighten us as to what secrets he's keeping."

A quick perusal of the writing desk and bookshelf turned up nothing. When they let themselves into the bedroom, however, Henry let out a short exclamation. "Ah ha!"

He snatched up a battered ledger, the cover spotted with mildew, from the corner of the washstand. "This was the book Thorpe took from the office."

As the curtains were drawn, Vincent risked turning on the gaslight, shutting the door to the sitting room so no suspicious light would show beneath the door to the hall. Crowding close enough to smell the fading remnants of Henry's bay rum cologne, Vincent peered over his shoulder as he opened the ledger.

Each page was divided into neat columns: NAME, AGE, DATE OF BIRTH, EFFECTS, and PSYCHICAL TALENT.

"It's a list of the orphans brought to Angel's Shadow," Vincent said. "But why would Thorpe want to conceal such a thing?"

"I can't imagine," Henry murmured. His brows drew together in concentration as he read off each name in turn. "Faith Morehouse. Quincy Brown. Pearl Smith. Sylvester Ortensi. Ramon Green. Ursula Thorpe." Henry's eyes widened behind the protective lenses of his spectacles. "A relative?"

"Perhaps an aunt? Thorpe said his father was in an orphanage as well. But I would have expected them to be in the same one."

"Unless his father didn't have any psychical talent," Henry said. "Whatever the case, her name wasn't on the plaque. She must have survived." He paged through the ledger, but the rest of it was blank. No doubt Mrs. Marsden had expected to fill them with the names of talented orphans as the years went on.

"Thorpe wanted to conceal this. But why? There's nothing of value here."

"Shame?" Vincent hazarded. "But no, that doesn't make any sense. He readily admitted to his adoption, and his father's. He even claimed their history was the reason he chose Angel's Shadow as the site of the investigation."

"Clearly he had other motives," Henry replied.

"Family secrets." Vincent's skin pricked with unease. "Always a nasty business."

"It would be nice to know more," Henry said, carefully replacing the ledger where they'd found it. "I'd hoped the ledger would...I don't know, contain something about the Grand Harmonium, or Xabat, or even some spiritual writings of Mrs. Marsden. Instead we have only more questions."

Vincent glanced at the door. "We should probably leave, before we press our luck too far."

As they spoke, the air in the room suddenly cooled. The flame of the gas lamp dimmed, as though something drew energy from it.

"Vincent?" Henry asked in alarm.

The taste of a fine cigar flooded Vincent's mouth. "It's the ghost." His heart lurched against his ribs, a mix of longing and anguish. "Dunne?"

A painting on the far wall suddenly swung askew, as though an unseen hand had pushed it.

Vincent didn't hesitate. Crossing the room, he lifted the painting from its hook, revealing a hidden cubbyhole. Possibly there had once been a safe there, but if so, it had been removed by some former occupant, leaving behind only a rough rectangle cut into the wall.

Perhaps satisfied with its work, the ghost's presence faded, then vanished altogether.

Vincent set the painting aside. Henry reached into the cubbyhole and drew out a box, its wood darkened with age. Neither spoke as he placed it on the bed and swung open the lid.

"What the devil is that?" Henry asked.

Vincent had no answer. A flat circle of black stone, only a bit bigger than his palm, lay within. Intricate carvings covered the surface, so fine and tiny it would take a magnifying glass to properly see them. The stone was set into a gold mount of some kind, as though it had been broken off something larger.

A sort of low buzz filled Vincent's skull. Not sound, not quite. More of a hum in his teeth, in the bones just below his ear, as though something resonated within him.

Henry nudged him and pointed to the inside of the box's lid. "Look at this."

A bit of paper, brown and brittle with age, had been wedged into the join. On it, written in a childish hand, was: *The Astral Key. Property of Ursula Thorpe.*

"I can't believe the two of you!" Lizzie exclaimed. "Breaking into Charles's room, searching through his things, like a pair of common hoodlums."

Vincent suppressed a sigh. Once again, the four of them had waited until the rest of the house settled. Rather than meet in Henry's chamber, they'd opted for Lizzie's, as it had a small sitting room attached. Vincent noted that Thorpe had given the best guest room in the women's wing to Lizzie, rather than Miss Blake or Jo.

He arched an eyebrow. "Charles, is it?"

A blush stained her cheeks. "None of your business, Vincent Night. And entirely beside the point."

"So Mr. Thorpe knows about the Grand Harmonium?" Jo asked. "But why didn't he say anything?"

"Does he, though?" Lizzie immediately countered. "You said the label only identified it as the Astral Key."

"The very thing Ortensi was searching for." Vincent restrained himself from rolling his eyes. "Thorpe wouldn't have brought it here with him for no reason."

Henry held up his hands. "We can hardly fault Mr. Thorpe for not telling us anything, given our own deception." He didn't point out they had been the ones to argue for it, but his deliberate pause was enough.

"What troubles me more is that Wellington implied our time here could be lucrative. And Mr. Thorpe felt the need to conceal the fact his aunt or grandmother had been at the orphanage. Combined with Ortensi's concerns that the Harmonium could be badly used…I'm very concerned."

"Perhaps Ursula Thorpe stole the Astral Key?" Lizzie suggested. "If Ortensi knew what had become of it, he and Dunne would have recovered it long ago. What do you think it does?"

Vincent shook his head slowly. "I don't know, but it has real power. I felt it buzzing in the air, almost."

"Did you?" Henry's pale brows drew together. "I sensed nothing at all."

Lizzie clasped her hands together. "Perhaps we should be more honest with Charles. Mention we've heard of the Grand Harmonium, if nothing else?"

Annoyance tugged at Vincent. "There's no reason to, any more than there was at the beginning. Dunne and Ortensi were both obsessed with keeping the Grand Harmonium secret. Ortensi at least believed it could be exploited for financial gain. Going by what he said to Henry our first evening here, Wellington intends to use it in such a fashion. An artifact, or a machine, that summons the dead with ease…I think the potential for misuse, for abuse of the departed, is clear."

"Then we have to expose Wellington to Charles," Lizzie said. "I know you're both unsure of him, but I don't believe Charles would be a party to anything corrupt."

Vincent bit back an argument. Lizzie was too smitten with Thorpe to listen to anything Vincent had to say.

He'd never seen her this way. Ordinarily she was the sensible one when it came to affairs of the heart. Thorpe was handsome, true, and charming. But something about him seemed to have cast an enchantment over her.

He glanced at Henry. Love wasn't sensible, or logical. It simply was.

"Exposing Wellington won't be easy." Henry sighed and took off his spectacles. Drawing out a handkerchief, he turned his attention to cleaning them, as if he wished to avoid everyone else's gaze. "It would seem Isaac—Wellington, I mean—has actual mediumistic talents after all."

Hell. Vincent put a hand on Henry's arm. "Are you certain? When Thorpe said our impressions of the spirit near the statue matched, I assumed Wellington had spoken vaguely enough for Mr. Thorpe's imagination to fill in."

"He wasn't vague at all," Henry said unhappily. "He identified the teacher quite clearly."

"Still, it might have been a lucky guess?" Vincent hazarded.

"No. He pointed out the cold spot from several feet away."

Blast the man. It somehow seemed doubly cruel, for him to possess a talent, which might have brought consolation to Henry's family, and refuse to use it even while taking everything from them.

"I'm sorry," Vincent said.

Henry put his spectacles back on. "No matter. The point is, if he deceived Thorpe, it wasn't with his talent. And if Thorpe showed him the Astral Key, as a medium he would likely have sensed its power as Vincent did. They know it's genuine, not simply a bit of carved stone."

"So long as Mr. Thorpe is working with such a snake, we can't trust him." Vincent paused, then added, "No matter how handsome and charming he might be."

He aimed the latter at Lizzie, who scowled at him. "Very well," she said at last.

"What I want to know is why the ghost from the mansion appeared at the orphanage," Henry said. "And then went so far as to reveal the hiding place of the Astral Key to us. It makes no sense."

Vincent drew a deep breath, his chest oddly tight. "It makes sense if the spirit is Dunne's." He lifted his gaze, found everyone else's gaze fixed on him. "Dunne knew me better than anyone except for Lizzie. All the secrets were on his side. Even if his spirit had returned to the orphanage for some reason, he might have sensed my presence in town."

Lizzie put a hand to her mouth. "And the Key? He hid the Grand Harmonium from us for years."

"Perhaps he's entrusting us to repair it."

"A bit late for that," Henry muttered.

Henry didn't understand. If Dunne was helping them, if he had visited Vincent in the night and moved against the nurse in the orphanage…perhaps he'd forgiven Vincent for killing him.

God.

Vincent reached into his coat and took out the slate with its damaged frame. "Mr. Thorpe isn't the only one who smuggled something out of the orphanage with no one else the wiser. I took this from the…I suppose we could call it the training room, on the third floor. Where the children practiced their talents." He passed it to Lizzie. "Look at the name on it."

"D. Marsden," Lizzie read. "So it either belonged to Dunne, or to his insane sister."

Vincent nodded. "Either way, we'll learn something."

"All right." She tucked a stray curl back from her face. "Let's get started."

# CHAPTER 10

"PSYCHOMETRY...OR spirit writing?" Lizzie asked.

Vincent spread his hands. "Those are your talents, not mine. What do you think would be best?"

She was silent for a long moment, bent over the slate. The gaslight softened her familiar profile. How often had he watched her at her work, just the tiniest line between her plucked brows? Thank God she was with him now. If he'd had to face Dunne's lies alone, he'd have fallen into despair weeks ago.

Not that he would have been alone. But Henry and Jo couldn't understand the depth of the relationship between apprentice and mentor. How far into his soul the betrayal left its mark.

"Spirit writing," she said at last. "If Dunne used this slate to do spirit writing of his own, it would be a powerful tool to contact him."

"Or Arabella," Jo said. "Maybe we can ask if she was the one who wrote on the chalkboard in the classroom." She shivered. "And how she knows my name."

"All right," Vincent said. "Everyone, you know what to do."

They had performed séances so many times at their shop or the homes of their clients, there was no longer any question as to who did what. Henry drew the curtains against the moonlight. Vincent moved the small side table into the center of the room and arranged the chairs around it. Jo lit a single candle, then extinguished the gaslights.

They sat in their usual arrangement around the table, hands joined. Vincent and Jo flanked Lizzie; as she needed her left hand free for writing, they both took her right hand. Henry's hand in Vincent's was firm, and Jo's face wore its familiar look of concentration, as though she sought to summon as much energy for the circle as possible.

A sense of calm spread through Vincent. Together, the four of them would find their way through this. Discover the Grand Harmonium and prevent anyone from using it for unscrupulous ends.

"I call upon the spirit of James Dunne, also known as James Marsden." Lizzie's voice remained utterly steady. "My hand is prepared to write your words. Draw from the energy of this circle and direct my hand as you will. I stand ready to receive you."

Lizzie set chalk to slate. Her eyes slipped closed, and her breath deepened as she slid into a trance.

For a long moment, Vincent feared nothing would happen. Then the lone candle flame turned blue and shrank in size. The air cooled rapidly, and Henry's hand tightened on his own.

Cigar smoke in his mouth. But this time, it mingled with river slime. With rot and blood.

What the devil?

Lizzie's left hand jerked. The chalk scratched wildly on the slate, the words sloppy, frantic.

*not her he's lying to you it be wasn't careful her son release me something else came*

What could it mean? "Spirit of James Dunne," Vincent said, putting as much command into his voice as he could. "Tell us what happened at Angel's Shadow Orphanage."

*if you can back instead have but save to your stop self it falling pain first*

The words were a jumble, utterly without meaning. The taste of rot intensified, almost blotting out the more wholesome cigars. "Where is the Grand Harmonium?" he tried.

*darkness cold have to stop I'm sorry it found him I love stopped you him*

"Vincent?" Jo asked worriedly.

"Don't break the circle," he ordered. What was going on? Why wasn't the writing clearer? The garbled words seemed to have no sense behind them, let alone any relation to the questions he asked.

"It isn't Dunne," he gasped. "It's Arabella. Lizzie, stop. This isn't working."

She didn't answer.

"Lizzie?"

*now I will stop YOU.*

The chalk flew across the room and struck the wall, even though Lizzie hadn't lifted her hand to throw it. Her head snapped back, mouth gaping open in a silent scream, entire body going stiff. The temperature plunged, their breath pluming like ectoplasm.

The taste of wet bone and slime, of decay and dank water flooded Vincent's mouth.

He knew this spirit. *Knew* it.

It was the ghost that had killed Dunne.

"Lizzie!" he shouted, wrenching his hands free and breaking the circle.

Lizzie's head jerked forward, eyes opening to show only blank white. A hideous snarl warped her lips.

"I will stop you," she said in a deep, growling voice utterly unlike her own. Her left hand snapped forward and closed around his throat.

"Vincent!" Henry cried, and lunged forward to grasp Lizzie's forearm. The muscles beneath her sleeve felt hard as iron. He struggled frantically to break her grip, but it was like fighting with a steel bar.

Vincent's face turned a dark shade of red, and he struggled for breath. His nails raked the back of the hand clenched around his throat, but Lizzie didn't so much as flinch. Instead, she rose to her feet, her chair clattering to the floor. Vincent's chair went over as well as she dragged him away from the table by his throat.

Henry abandoned his futile attempts to pry her free. His heart pounded in his ears, and bile coated the back of his throat. Arabella's ghost meant to kill Vincent right in front of them using Lizzie's body. Even now, Vincent's struggles seemed to grow more and more feeble.

No. This couldn't happen. Henry couldn't stand here and watch the man he loved die.

Henry snatched up a chair and hit Lizzie as hard as he could across her shoulders. Jo let out a shriek, but the blow didn't seem to make any difference at all.

The door burst open, and Miss Blake charged in, wearing a nightshirt and robe. "What the—" she started—then stopped at the sight of Lizzie. "Oh hell."

"Don't just stand there, help us!" Henry yelled.

Miss Blake lifted her hand, pointing at Lizzie's form. "I command you, spirit, to leave this woman and trouble her no more!"

To Henry's surprise, Lizzie staggered slightly, as though Miss Blake had landed a blow. Vincent wrenched free and collapsed to the floor, gagging and gasping.

Lizzie turned to face Miss Blake, her eyes still white blanks in her face. "I will stop you," she growled. "Xabat will not succeed!"

There came the clatter of footsteps in the hall. Thorpe flung himself through the door, a poker clutched in his hand, his hair in disarray and a robe tied loosely over his nightshirt. At the sight of Lizzie, his mouth gaped open in horror. "Elizabeth?"

"Get back!" Jo cried. "She's possessed!"

Henry dropped to his knees beside Vincent. "Are you all right?"

"The amulet," Vincent croaked. He pulled the silver chain over his head and pressed it into Henry's hand.

Lizzie's lips drew back from her teeth. She moved toward Thorpe, her hands twisted into claws. "The Grand Harmonium must not be restored," she said. "I drove back Xabat once before, and I will again. Which means you have to die."

The silver chain was so cold it burned Henry's fingers. Silently praying the amulet would work on someone already possessed, he tossed it over Lizzie's head.

She jerked, as though he'd cast a net about her. Her back arched, neck bending painfully back until her white gaze met Henry's. A furious growl escaped her, and for a horrible moment Henry felt as though Arabella's ghost looked straight into him. Marked him as her enemy.

Some tension seemed to snap. Lizzie's eyes shut, and she collapsed bonelessly into Thorpe's arms.

"Elizabeth!" he cried in alarm.

Her eyes fluttered. "Charles?" she whispered. Then she gasped, eyes widening. "Oh God. Vincent!"

Henry hurried back to Vincent. His color had returned to normal, but red marks stood out on his throat. By tomorrow, they'd doubtless look even worse.

Henry's hands shook with reaction. He wanted nothing more than to clasp Vincent to him, whisper how much he loved him, how terrified he'd been.

But Thorpe was watching. So instead, he put a steadying hand to Vincent's shoulder. "What can I get you? Tea? Water?"

"I'm fine." His voice rasped. "Well, not fine. I'm very much the opposite of fine." He swallowed convulsively. "The spirit...Arabella... I've encountered her before. She was the ghost that possessed me in New York and murdered Dunne."

Here. It—she—was here.

All the months he'd spent afraid the malevolent ghost would catch up with him, telling himself his fears were folly, they would never come true. The spirit had killed Dunne and departed, and it couldn't possibly be hunting him.

He should have listened to his fears. Should have...should have...

Henry's hand was a solid weight on his shoulder. Vincent swallowed, and swallowed again. Tremors ran through him, and he felt helpless to stop them. His hands quivered as he took out his tin of cachous, shook a pile into his hand, and popped them all into his mouth at once. The cinnamon burned against his tongue, but it didn't matter. Anything to blot out the aftertaste of slime and blood.

"Dunne?" Thorpe asked. "That was the name of Mrs. Marsden's first husband."

God. All their carefully constructed lies were about to fall apart, and Vincent couldn't even bring himself to care.

"Arabella killed Dunne," Vincent said through numb lips. His head spun.

"Just as she killed the rest of her family," Lizzie said tiredly. "I never imagined she would be so strong. Why was she so strong?"

Henry's grip tightened on Vincent's shoulder. "Jo, could you fetch blankets for Vincent and Lizzie, please?"

There came the whisper of skirts, retreating to Lizzie's bedroom, then returning. A comforting weight settled around Vincent's shoulders. "There you go," Henry said. "You're all right."

He wasn't, though. "Lizzie, if I'd known...if I'd guessed, I would never have suggested the spirit writing. I'm so sorry. This is my fault."

Lizzie slumped in a chair, while Thorpe tucked a second blanket around her. Her skin had gone bone white, and she shivered visibly.

Vincent remembered the cold the spirit brought with it. Not just external, but soul-deep. The exhaustion, as though he'd spent hours holding up a weight almost too heavy to bear.

Hurt showed in Thorpe's dark eyes as he focused on Lizzie. "Elizabeth? You know something about James Dunne Marsden?"

The appearance of the spirit—of Arabella—made it too dangerous to keep secrets any longer. Vincent knew it. And so did Lizzie.

"He...was our mentor," she said. "I'm sorry, Charles. So much has happened...we didn't know who to trust." She tugged the blanket more tightly about her. "Dunne—Marsden—lied to us. There were other apprentices who died, and if he couldn't be trusted, who could?"

Thorpe took her hands and began to chafe her fingers to warm them. "Just tell me what's happening here. You said the ghost was Arabella? The one who murdered all those people, at least according to the plaque?"

"She killed Dunne in New York." Vincent lowered his eyes to his lap, grateful for the blanket's warmth. "I was with him when he died."

"But why?" Thorpe asked, confused. "And what did she mean when she said she drove Xabat back once before? Do you believe her murder of her mother was somehow connected to her paranoia about the spirit guide?"

Arabella had betrayed them. Something had happened to the Grand Harmonium, something Ortensi and Dunne had spent their lives trying to undo. Had she sabotaged it in some fashion?

It took a great deal of fury and pain to create a ghost so powerful. How had she died? And why was she willing to kill to keep the Grand Harmonium from being restored?

"Would someone please explain what's going on?" Miss Blake demanded. "Why were you trying to raise your mentor? And what the devil is the Grand Harmonium?"

"We don't know." Vincent licked desert-dry lips. "We didn't even know Dunne had owned Angel's Shadow. We believed he'd been an orphan here, along with Sylvester Ortensi." If Dunne hadn't died, would he ever have told them? "Last year, a violent ghost—his sister, it would seem—murdered him. Afterwards, everything came apart. We discovered he and Ortensi had lied to us. They'd been working to restore something called the Grand Harmonium. Supposedly it calls upon the dead in some fashion, far more easily than ordinary mediumship. But we don't know the details, or why they were so determined to rebuild it."

"I saw Mr. Thorpe's letter in the Baltimore Psychical Society's journal," Henry put in. "It seemed the opportunity for Vincent and Lizzie to find the answers they sought."

"It was a sign." Vincent glanced up and met Miss Blake's gaze. "You said you'd had a strong feeling and encouraged Mr. Thorpe to advertise in Baltimore. You were right."

Dunne wanted them to find the Harmonium. He'd revealed the Astral Key, perhaps even guided Miss Blake in some fashion.

"When we came here, we only knew Dunne and Ortensi had been orphans and grown up in this orphanage." Lizzie put her fingertips to her eyes tiredly. "We had no idea Dunne's parents were superintendent and matron, or that he had a sister."

"Whose ghost somehow found him in New York and murdered him?" Miss Blake scratched her head. "I suppose she might have been able to travel to him thanks to their shared blood, but why wait forty years to do it?"

Henry slipped his arm around Vincent's shoulders. "Ortensi's journal suggests he believed the Grand Harmonium could be turned to… less than honorable purposes," Henry said carefully. "It seemed foolish to speak of it openly, when we knew next to nothing about it."

Lizzie gazed up at Thorpe with a pleading expression on her face. "You understand, don't you, Charles? Why we feared to say anything, with so much in question?"

Frightened and dismayed as he was, Vincent still had to admire Lizzie. She'd just put Thorpe neatly in a bind, as he'd been hiding information from them as well.

A struggle showed briefly in Thorpe's eyes. Then he nodded. "I do understand. I fear you're not the only ones who have been keeping secrets."

"The devil?" Miss Blake folded her arms over her chest. "Am I the only person here who isn't lying through her teeth?"

"I beg your pardon, Miss Blake," Thorpe said with a small bow in her direction. "But don't you see? Your intuition brought us all here together for a reason. I'm more convinced of it than ever." He turned back to Lizzie. "Forgive me, Elizabeth, for not trusting to fate from the start. The spirits tried to communicate through Miss Blake, but I was unwilling to take their message entirely to heart. But no more." He took a deep breath. "I have a connection with Angel's Shadow as well, much like your own. My father, Ulysses Thorpe, was one of the orphans."

*Father.* But the name in the ledger had been Ursula, not Ulysses. Vincent had assumed the name to belong to an aunt, but it sounded as though they'd been the same person. Had Ursula Thorpe become Ulysses Thorpe at some point? Perhaps during the war, when so many had cut off their hair and exchanged skirts for a uniform and rifle?

If so, Charles's own adoption years later might not have been legal. The marriage between his adoptive parents certainly wouldn't have been, and a clever lawyer could cast enough doubt in the minds of a jury to rule Charles had no right to inherit the small empire built by Ulysses Thorpe.

At least it explained why he'd concealed the ledger. It was likely the last bit of evidence that could prove Ulysses had once been known as Ursula. Hopefully he had enough sense to burn it, before someone like Wellington found it.

Vincent glanced at Henry, who had started to open his mouth. He shut it abruptly an instant later, no doubt coming to the same conclusion as Vincent had.

"Father left me something, when he passed," Thorpe went on. "I believe it to be a part of this Grand Harmonium you speak of." He looked from Lizzie's pale face to Vincent's. "But perhaps we should discuss this tomorrow, once you've had a chance to rest, and I've explained things to Mr. Wellington. It was his suggestion we keep the knowledge of the Grand Harmonium between the two of us."

"I'll bet it was," Henry muttered. "Here, Vincent. Let me help you back to your room."

Vincent felt as though he'd aged ten years in an hour. "Everyone, salt your windows and doors. In case it—she—comes back."

"Can she, though?" Miss Blake asked. "Without being summoned?"

Hadn't she seen the violence? The fear? "If you want to take the chance, be my guest."

"Easy there." Henry helped Vincent to his feet. "It hurts nothing as a precaution, Miss Blake. Especially if Arabella is looking for more mediums to possess."

Her mouth twisted sourly. "You have a point."

"At least it seems unlikely Arabella was the one to write the message on the chalkboard earlier today," Henry added. "That spirit was much weaker—it seemed barely able to manipulate the chalk."

"You're right," Jo said, sounding relieved. "Maybe it was one of the children after all."

Vincent and Henry started for the door. "Vincent?" Lizzie called uncertainly. "Are you all right? I didn't mean to…."

Guilt flashed through him. He knew better than anyone what she was going through, and yet he'd said not a supportive word. "I know." He put a hand to her shoulder as they stopped by her chair. "You never blamed me for Dunne's death. Don't blame yourself for this." He glanced at Miss Blake. "I'm sorry to have snapped at you. But this ghost…" He shook his head. "She murdered my mentor with my own hands. Do you understand?"

She flinched. "I…yes. I'm sorry."

Henry walked quietly beside Vincent, back to the men's wing. They passed Vincent's chamber and went by unspoken consent to Henry's door. The household around them was silent; there was no one to see.

"Don't worry," Henry said. "We'll stop Arabella. Somehow."

Vincent shook his head. She was so strong. And now she'd found him again… "That's just it, Henry. I'm not certain we can."

# CHAPTER 11

Vincent didn't sleep at all the rest of the night. Henry curled around him, holding him tight, offering what comfort he could with his presence. Whispering to Vincent, over and over again: "I love you. You're safe. I won't let anything happen to you."

It helped. He clasped Henry's hand with his own, held it to his chest, where they could both feel the beating of his heart. Breathed in Henry's familiar scent, as they both lay awake through the small hours.

But nothing could banish the sense of dread suffocating Vincent's heart, the same way the ghost had tried to suffocate his lungs.

The horror of the night Dunne died replayed over and over again in his mind. They'd had a small occult shop in New York, and Dunne's long residency meant people in the neighborhood knew who to turn to when they had troubling encounters with ghosts. So when a man came to ask for help with a poltergeist, nothing had seemed out of the ordinary.

Poltergeists were simple spirits, most of them with no remaining personality or thoughts of their own. They mindlessly fed off the fear and frustration of the living, usually fastening onto the higher energy available from a child. Eventually, the poltergeist would grow strong enough to pinch people, or throw objects—anything to frighten the living, so it could further feast on their energy and become even more powerful.

This poltergeist had already reached the stage of tossing around furniture. Even so, such beings weren't typically difficult for an experienced medium to remove. As Lizzie already had an appointment to conduct a séance elsewhere, Vincent and Dunne went to the house. Never thinking for a moment one of them wouldn't return.

But the ghost lurking in the house hadn't been a poltergeist, but a thing with intelligence. It possessed Vincent completely and used his hands to strangle Dunne.

If only Vincent had no memory of the event. He didn't want to recall Dunne gasping ineffective commands at the spirit to leave Vincent's body. Or the way he'd torn at Vincent's grip, struggling for his life.

Least of all how his throat had felt, cartilage buckling beneath Vincent's fingers. His skin going from warm to cold.

In the morning, Vincent awoke drained. The spirit had used him and moved on, leaving him beside the body of the man who had been like a father to him.

And now, to find out the ghost belonged to Dunne's own sister? That she had become this creature of hate and horror, of cold water and wet bone?

Had she died on Angel Mountain? She'd murdered her mother and stepfather, along with the orphanage staff and several other children. Clearly her obsession had followed her into death…but why had she waited so long, traveled so far, to strike Dunne at last?

God, she was strong. Powerful ghosts usually had two things in common: they'd had forceful personalities when alive, and their passing hadn't been easy.

But Dunne was here, too. In the taste of cigars, the feeling of warmth and comfort. Vincent had sensed him for a few moments, before Arabella took over. Had he tried to protect them, as he'd tried to protect them from the nurse's ghost? As he'd shown them where the Astral Key was concealed inside Thorpe's room?

Vincent held up his hands. In the predawn light, he could just make out each finger. These hands had killed Dunne. Despite everything they'd learned about the man in the last few months, he couldn't shake the feeling he still owed his mentor.

If they restored the Grand Harmonium, perhaps Vincent could use it to finally speak to Dunne beyond the veil. Finally get the answers he so desperately craved.

Maybe then they could both be at peace.

As the light grew stronger, Vincent slipped out of Henry's bed and retreated to his room. He splashed water on his face and winced at the sight of the dark rings around his eyes. Not to mention the purple bruises around his throat. Even swallowing hurt. As he dressed, a door creaked open and footsteps passed by. Wellington, no doubt, who had slept through the commotion of the night before.

Of course, the man had told Thorpe to keep the Grand Harmonium a secret. Vincent imagined his reaction to learning everyone now knew, and smirked.

A short while later, Henry knocked on his door. "Did you manage to sleep at all?" he asked.

Vincent finished knotting his tie. "Obvious, is it?"

Henry put his hands on Vincent's hips, looking up at him. "How are you?" Concern shone from his blue eyes. "Last night must have been terrible. Encountering that spirit—Arabella—again, after it hurt you so the first time."

Vincent's chest ached with love, and he found one corner of his mouth turning up into a faint smile. Henry had held him so fiercely last night, as if he meant to protect Vincent from her spirit with his own body. "I can't say I'm happy about it. But I'm not going to fall apart, either. It helps, having you here."

Henry caught Vincent's hand and brought it to his lips. "Then I'm glad to be here. Shall we try some breakfast?"

Vincent's stomach cramped at the thought, but he forced himself to nod. He'd need his energy, no matter what happened later.

Jo, Lizzie, and Miss Blake were already at breakfast. Lizzie seemed surprisingly serene, and a little smile played around her lips, no doubt in response to some internal thought. When she caught sight of Vincent, however, her face fell. "Vincent, your neck."

Fortunately his collar hid most of the bruising, but couldn't cover it entirely. "It's nothing," he said.

"Still, I'm sorry. Would you like your amulet back?"

"So long as you aren't planning on any more spirit writing."

"Definitely not." She removed the necklace and passed it back to him.

He caught her hand as she did so. "And you? How are you feeling?"

He remembered all too well how he'd felt, the morning after being possessed. Cold and exhaustion had been his first sensations, followed quickly by horror. Grief and guilt and stinging shame.

To his surprise, a second smile curved her mouth. "Well, actually. Better than I have any right to."

Vincent leaned in and put his mouth near her ear. "I see. And does

Mr. Thorpe have anything to do with this? I *thought* I heard footfalls in the hall at a rather late hour…"

"A lady never tells," she said, giving him a stern look. Which was confirmation enough.

"Of course not." He gave her a quick kiss on the cheek and pulled away. "Where is Mr. Thorpe now, by the way?"

"Charles and Mr. Wellington stepped out to speak alone. They—"

The tread of footsteps interrupted her. "It's too late," Thorpe said as he entered the breakfast room. "And the decision was mine to make, not yours."

Wellington followed on his heels, an unpleasant expression on his face. Henry stiffened at Vincent's side. "It was irresponsible of you to say anything without consulting me."

Thorpe came to a halt, turning on his heel so Wellington nearly walked into him. "As I said, it was my choice to make, Mr. Wellington." His voice cooled the air almost as efficiently as a ghost. "Arguing with me now will change nothing."

Wellington opened his mouth, as if to disagree. As he did so, however, his gaze strayed to Henry.

His mouth shut with a snap. "Of course, Charles. You're quite right. Forgive me if I overstepped my bounds. I'm certain you've made the right decision by telling our friends."

Vincent didn't care for the change of heart at all. He slipped into one of the chairs at the table, and Henry sat by him. Thorpe took a chair by Lizzie before ringing the bell. Servants whisked in, laying plates out for everyone who had just entered and—more importantly, in Vincent's opinion—pouring steaming mugs of coffee. "If you could just leave the carafe," Thorpe said. "Thank you."

The servants retreated. Henry tucked into his scrambled eggs. Wellington spread jam over a piece of toast, all traces of his earlier temper hidden away. Thorpe only stared at his plate, as if the maple syrup on his pancakes spelled out a message.

"You said your father had left you something connected with the Grand Harmonium," Vincent said, as though he and Henry hadn't already seen it. Henry went an odd color of puce and busied himself with his eggs. "Would you care to elaborate?"

Thorpe picked up his own coffee, then put it back down without tasting it. "You must understand. My father never spoke of his time at Angel's Shadow. I knew nothing of the orphanage, of the Grand Harmonium. I didn't even know he had mediumistic talents. I assume

Father meant to take the story to his grave. Until my mother died." Thorpe swallowed. "He loved her, you see. He summoned me to him, showed me the contents of a box, and swore me to secrecy. Though it's far too late for that now."

Lizzie laid her fingers on the skin of his wrist, just above the cuff. Thorpe seemed to rally at her touch. "Father said the Astral Key had been part of a machine called the Grand Harmonium, built by the staff of the first orphanage he was in. He said he'd taken it—hidden it— because he'd seen firsthand the strife it caused. It was the sort of thing men would kill for."

Vincent sat up sharply. "Kill for?"

"Indeed." Thorpe raised his gaze, his face drawn, as though he, too, had slept not at all. "It isn't merely a method of communication with the spirit world, more reliable than mediumship, as you surmised. It does something which men have dreamed of throughout the ages. The Grand Harmonium restores the dead to life."

"That's not possible," Vincent said. "It...it can't be."

Henry surreptitiously slipped his hand beneath the table cloth and laid it on Vincent's knee. He'd never seen Vincent as frightened as he'd been last night. And all Henry had been able to do was press his skin to Vincent's, and helplessly whisper endearments and promises in the dark.

"I told you they'd say that," Wellington said, giving Thorpe a pointed look. "This is one of the reasons we agreed to keep it private. No one else will believe you."

Anger bubbled in Henry's chest. The words were different than the ones Wellington had spoken to him so long ago, and yet the sentiment was the same. *I'm the only one you can trust. Ignore the naysayers.*

"I say let's hear Mr. Thorpe out," he said, casting Wellington a defiant glare.

Thorpe seemed surprised at the forcefulness of Henry's words. "Thank you, Mr. Strauss. I know it sounds impossible. To return the dead to a living state, flesh and blood once again...it sounded like raving to me when Father spoke of it. I thought he'd become unhinged by grief. When I suggested as much, he grew furious, and...and we quarreled." Thorpe swallowed heavily. "We parted in anger. I departed for Newport and raced yachts with my friends. Went to parties. Lived as though no care existed in the world. Until I received the telegram stating my father was dead."

"I'm sorry," Lizzie said. "It must have been difficult for you."

Thorpe pushed away his plate, abandoning all pretext of eating. "It was. The servants told me he'd tried a séance. The most trusted of them sat with him, with the Astral Key before him on the table. He was attempting to contact Mr. Marsden, to ask for guidance."

"Not Mrs. Marsden?" Henry asked with a frown. "Wasn't she the one making most of the decisions here?"

Thorpe spread his hands apart. "I don't know. Apparently after the séance began, something went wrong. Father went rigid—then tore free of the circle, rushed into the hall, and flung himself over the balcony."

Ice water seemed to trickle down Henry's spine. Beside him, Vincent's skin took on a grayish hue. "Might Arabella have killed him?" Vincent said. "Possessed him as she possessed Lizzie and me, only he was her target and not merely her vessel."

"Could she have some special connection with the other orphans, which would lead her to them?" Lizzie leaned back and tapped a nail against the side of her coffee mug thoughtfully. "Though she never troubled Ortensi."

"At a guess, her connection was with the Astral Key. And her link with Dunne through their blood." Vincent took a sip of his coffee and made a face. Reaching for more sugar, he added, "And we were the fools who summoned her with her own spirit writing slate."

"So she can't just…reach out and attack us?" Miss Blake asked hopefully. "I'd feel a lot better if I knew there wasn't a spirit waiting to pounce."

"I didn't know—don't know, really—what happened to Father. I thought he'd had some sort of fit…but if he was murdered by Arabella…" Thorpe shook his head. "I'd abandoned him to his grief. Let him down when he needed me the most. So I decided to find out if he was right. If the Grand Harmonium could truly bring him and Mother back to life. I took the Astral Key to Ira here." He nodded at Wellington. "He was able to tell me it had a connection with the other side. That spirits could pass through it."

Could it be true? Henry's first instinct was to dismiss anything Wellington said as nonsense. But Vincent had perceived some sort of power from the device. Perhaps the only people Wellington had ever set out to deceive were Henry and his mother.

"We've spent the last several months attempting to find out more," Thorpe said. "I couldn't believe my luck when I saw Angel's Shadow was available for sale. I took it as a sign."

"It was," Vincent said firmly. "Just as your letter in the psychical journal was a sign to us. Now that everything is out in the open, I suggest we join forces. The Grand Harmonium must be near the orphanage, somewhere. Let's return there and direct all of our efforts toward finding and restoring it."

Henry blinked. He'd expected a bit of discussion, if nothing else. "Is such a course of action truly wise? Even if it works as it's meant to, should we use it?"

"Have you never lost anyone you'd give anything to see again, Mr. Strauss?" Thorpe asked.

Henry glanced at Wellington—then cursed himself. Wellington had been a fraud, or had behaved as one, and taken everything. But if he had truly been able to bring Henry's father back to life, wouldn't it have been a good thing?

Still, the thought sat uneasily with him. "Your own father warned you people would kill for this sort of power," he said carefully.

"Which is why it must be kept secret," Wellington replied, glaring at Thorpe as he did so.

Lizzie glanced from Thorpe to Vincent, her brows drawn together. "I agree with Henry. We need to at least discuss the wisdom of restoring the Grand Harmonium, let alone using it."

Some of the color drained from Vincent's sienna skin. "What is there to discuss?" he demanded.

"Think, Vincent!" Lizzie's expression sharpened to a glare. "There's a natural order to things. Our duty is to help the dead rest peacefully. What you're proposing is the opposite, dragging those who have passed on to the other side back to our world! Necromancy, in other words."

"It isn't necromancy! We wouldn't be controlling their spirits. We'd be restoring them to flesh and blood."

Miss Blake cleared her throat loudly. "With all due respect, Miss Devereaux, if the Grand Harmonium does what Mr. Thorpe's father claimed, it would change the world. I understand what you mean about disturbing the dead who have made their peace and passed on," she added, holding up a hand before Lizzie could reply. "But think about it. Mrs. Marsden was guided by a spirit."

"Xabat," Thorpe put in helpfully.

The scrambled eggs sat queasily in Henry's belly. "Arabella seemed afraid of Xabat."

Miss Blake frowned. "Arabella also killed almost everyone who was at the orphanage. Her mind was obviously disturbed, and she interpreted benign protection as some sort of malevolent surveillance."

"And the writing on the chalkboard?" Henry challenged.

"Might not even refer to Xabat."

"She's right, Henry," Vincent said. "What were you going to say, Miss Blake?"

"Xabat brought Mrs. Marsden to these hills, told her where to build the orphanage. I don't think it's a stretch to imagine he instructed her to build the Grand Harmonium." She looked first at Henry, then at Lizzie. "If that's so...have you stopped to think perhaps the spirits themselves want this to happen? What if it's the next step in humanity's journey?" Her eyes all but shone. "Can you imagine bringing back the great thinkers of the past? Aristotle, Alexander the Great, Francis Bacon—brilliant minds enlightened even further from their time in the world beyond."

"*'We would have made the world a paradise.'*," Vincent quoted Ortensi's journal. "Think of it, Henry! Imagine what you could learn speaking with them."

For a moment, Henry could see the potential. What secrets might the great men and women of history, working together, uncover? What had they perhaps already uncovered on the other side, and were finally ready to share with the living?

He'd let himself get swept away with heady notions before. Acted without thinking. Each time had ended only in grief.

"I just don't think we should rush into this," he said at last. "We have too many questions."

"Which we could answer easily!" Vincent struck his palm against the table. "We've spent months wondering about Dunne and Ortensi. If they loved us at all. If everything was just a lie."

"Vincent," Lizzie said softly.

Anguish filled Vincent's dark eyes. "If we could have answers, real answers...if I could tell Dunne I didn't mean to kill him, that I was possessed." Vincent touched the bruises around his own throat. "With the Grand Harmonium, I could undo what happened."

Henry's ribs seemed to squeeze his heart. He wished he might take Vincent in his arms. Kiss his shining black hair and tell him everything was going to be all right.

"I vote we restore the Harmonium," Jo said in a small voice.

She'd been so quiet, Henry had nearly forgotten her presence. "Jo?"

"My parents would want to come back, wouldn't they?" she asked. "They never meant to leave me alone. If I could just see them again." Tears collected on her lashes. "Please, Henry? Can't we at least try?"

"You don't have to come, if you're truly set against this, Henry,"

Vincent said. Struggling to be reasonable, no doubt. "You and Lizzie can stay here."

"Don't be absurd," Lizzie snapped.

Henry sighed. "We're partners. Where you go, I go."

Happiness bloomed over Vincent's face. Jo squealed and hugged him.

"There's only one problem." Lizzie leaned back in her chair. "We have no idea where the Grand Harmonium is."

"The basement?" Thorpe guessed. "Perhaps we could search for the entrance."

"Or we could try asking someone who knows," Vincent said. "If we held a séance in the orphanage, we might make contact with Everett or the nurse. Or even one of the children."

"Or Arabella," Henry said darkly.

"I sensed the nurse feared we'd harm something, but not one of her charges," Wellington put in. "What if she and the ghost of Mr. Everett have been guarding the Grand Harmonium all these years? Keeping out anyone who might find or destroy it."

It made sense. And it would explain why Dunne and Ortensi had been granted safe passage for their repairs. The ghosts knew them, understood what they were about.

"After last night, I think we all can agree to be cautious when it comes to séances," Henry said. "It's too dangerous to risk any of our mediums." A part of him still felt uncertain, but he feared Vincent would risk himself if Henry didn't offer an alternative. "We'll use the Electro-Séance instead. That will hopefully prevent Arabella from possessing anyone, should she decide to join us."

"Excellent idea." Thorpe came to his feet, seeming invigorated. "Is there anything you need to do here to prepare?"

Stalling would only mean fewer hours of daylight left to use. Though daylight hadn't exactly kept them safe so far. "No." Henry suppressed a heavy sigh. "Let's go to the orphanage and get this over with."

# CHAPTER 12

"May I speak with you, Henry?" Wellington called through Henry's door.

Henry's shoulders tensed. He'd gone to his room with the intention of changing into something more suitable for exploring a dank basement than the clothes he'd worn to breakfast. Wellington must have followed him up.

He straightened his tie before yanking the door open, positioning himself to block Wellington from coming inside. "What do you want?"

Wellington glanced up and down the hall, but it was empty. "May I come in?"

The thought of being alone with Wellington again made Henry's skin crawl. "No."

"As you wish. Everyone else is still downstairs, so it makes no matter." Wellington made a show of straightening his cuffs. "I simply wished to speak with you privately before we depart for the orphanage. About the Grand Harmonium."

Things slipped into place. "The Harmonium is why you didn't object to Thorpe hiring me. You want me to repair it."

"If need be, yes." Wellington tilted his head to one side. "Charles and Mr. Night are blinded by their desire to make amends with the dead. Miss Blake is a true Spiritualist who believes all that rot about bettering the lot of humanity."

Henry's skin itched, as if bees swarmed underneath. So close, he could smell Wellington's cologne—not the same scent as he'd worn all those years ago, thank God. Even so, he didn't want it in his lungs. "And you? I assume this is the financial benefit you spoke of earlier."

"Think of it, Henry." Wellington crowded in closer, forcing Henry to step back into the room. "Unlike Mr. Night and Mr. Thorpe, you and I aren't fixated on the past. We can see the future potential of the Grand Harmonium."

Henry struggled to keep his face expressionless. "Mr. Thorpe owns the land and everything on it. You should be trying to convince him, not me."

"I intend to." Wellington paused. "Between the two of us, however, we might even be able to construct a second one. Imagine it. Imagine what those who can afford it might pay to have their loved ones return."

Acid stung Henry's throat. "You sicken me."

Wellington's eyes narrowed. "You're allowing our past history to cloud your thinking."

"The way you let your mother's foolish accusations cloud yours? The way you decided if you couldn't have revenge against Father directly, you'd have it on those he loved?" Henry was the one to step forward this time. "I despise you and everything you stand for. I wouldn't assist you for all the money in the world."

Wellington gave way. "Don't be a fool." His lip curled slightly as he retreated to the hall. "If the Harmonium is restored, what place do you imagine there will be for trinkets like your Electro-Séance? Or even the workings of other mediums? You and your friends won't fare well in the new order of things. You're either with me…or not. And I promise, you don't want me as your enemy."

Vincent leaned forward as the wagon made its slow way up the overgrown path to the orphanage. Beside him, Jo nearly vibrated with excitement.

"Can't we go any faster?" she asked.

"And what? Run up on the carriage?" Henry gestured to the conveyance in front of them. "We'll get there soon enough."

Henry had barely glanced at either of them the entire ride up the mountainside. Displeased they hadn't listened to him and Lizzie, Vincent surmised.

Henry didn't understand, that was all. His memory of how eager he'd been to contact his father again was blighted by Wellington's betrayal. He couldn't see this was entirely different.

He couldn't see this was Vincent's only chance to wash the blood from his hands.

How the Grand Harmonium actually operated, Vincent couldn't guess. Henry and Jo were clever, though; with their help, they'd be able to restore the machine and make things right. Jo would have her parents again. Vincent would finally be able to get the answers he needed from Dunne.

Dunne would be able to forgive him.

Vincent put his hand to Henry's knee. "Thank you for agreeing to do the Electro-Séance."

Henry glanced at him...and his expression softened. "I love you. I know this means a great deal to you. And I hope my concerns are unfounded."

"Ortensi said it would bring about paradise. I think Miss Blake has the right of it—once it's operational, we'll be able to reach anyone on the other side and benefit from their wisdom. Restore them to life, so they can create and build with their own hands. Imagine new paintings from Leonardo DaVinci, or sculptures from Michaelangelo." Vincent took a deep breath. "I don't agree with what Ortensi was trying to do in Devil's Walk, and I certainly wish they'd taken us into their confidence...but if Dunne's own sister murdered his mother and stepfather, I can understand why they lied to us. Given her ghost's fixation on preventing us from restoring the Grand Harmonium, her betrayal likely had some relation to its construction. Perhaps she was even the reason they had to restore it, if she chose sabotage. There was too much at stake to fail a second time." He stared off into the woods. "I believe perhaps Lizzie and I judged too harshly."

"Ortensi tried to kill us!" Henry shook his head. "And Dunne's previous apprentices died. I don't think you could judge them too harshly."

"We don't know for certain what happened to the other apprentices," Vincent pointed out. "Ortensi took things too far at the end, but that wasn't Dunne's doing. And don't forget, Dunne's been protecting us since we arrived."

Henry's lips tightened until they turned as white as the rest of his skin. Jo put a hand on his arm. "Just think, Henry. You can finally meet Mama. You'd like that, wouldn't you?"

"Of course I would," Henry said immediately. "I regret making no attempt to contact your family once I reached my majority, more than almost any other mistake I've made."

It wasn't exactly a truce, but close enough. The rest of the ride continued in silence, until they were again gathered before the orphanage.

Thorpe held the box containing the Astral Key. "Where shall we set up our séance—and which ghost shall we communicate with?"

"Not the nurse," Miss Blake said. "She seemed like she was in a bad mood. Best leave her alone."

Vincent put his hand to his chin in thought. "The children may not be the most useful. They would know less than the adults, no doubt. And be more easily distracted."

Lizzie shifted from foot to foot. "Which leaves the teacher."

"The classroom would be the logical choice of location." Henry peered at the orphanage like a general studying the lay of the land for a battle.

"Perhaps I'd feel better about all this if we knew exactly what happened all those years ago." Lizzie folded her arms over her chest. "How so many died, including Arabella. Why Dunne, Ortensi, and Ulysses survived."

"That should be one of the first questions we ask the spirit," Henry replied. "All right. No sense delaying any longer."

They poured a line of salt across the doorway to the classroom. Once it was in place, Wellington broke the salt line in front of the angel statue to release the ghost, then hurried back. Vincent helped Henry and Jo set up the Electro-Séance, while the rest watched with interest. The lack of any light save for the dim lanterns slowed the process, but they needed to preserve the batteries of the arc lights, in case the spirit grew violent.

"What are all these gadgets of yours for, Mr. Strauss?" Miss Blake asked curiously.

Henry appeared less pleased than usual at the opportunity to show off his equipment. "The Wimshurst Machine will provide electro-magnetic energy to whatever spirit is drawn here. Once it has manifested, we will use the phantom fence to trap it." He pointed at an arrangement of wooden fence posts linked by several strands of copper wire. "The ends of the wires are connected to a battery, which we'll cover in salt to keep the spirit from draining them. The electric charge thus formed will prevent the spirit from passing through the fence. If the ghost turns violent, it will be contained and unable to reach anyone else."

"Except for the person cranking the Wimshurst Machine," Jo put in. "They'll be stuck inside the fence with the ghost."

"Which is why I always conduct the séance myself," Henry said. "If things should go wrong, we have the dispeller, which uses water and a piezo-electric crystal to humidify the air. Electric charges, including those comprising spirits, are better conducted in dry air than damp. I will also have the ghost grounder. The copper rod has the ability to drain the ghost's electric charge—its energy, if you will."

"Don't forget the arc light," Jo added. She was busy setting it up well away from anything flammable, so its heat wouldn't start a fire. "Ghosts hate it. If Henry gets into a bad situation, I'll connect the arc light to the batteries and chase the spirit off."

"Very impressive," Wellington said. Henry made no reply.

"What about communicating with the ghost?" Miss Blake asked. "Usually in a séance they use the medium's voice to speak, or hand to write."

"As strong as these ghosts are already, with the additional energy provided by the Wimshurst Machine, I suspect he will be able to communicate more directly." Henry carefully checked the security of the fence wires. "If not, we'll resort to asking him to rap on the floor."

"Which medium shall ask the questions?" Thorpe asked.

"I will," Lizzie offered. Vincent cast her a startled look, and she shrugged. "In for a penny, in for a pound."

Soon enough the elements of the Electro-Séance were in place. Vincent put a hand to Henry's elbow. "Perhaps I should join you inside the fence. Just in case someone unexpected answers your call."

Henry offered him a small smile. "No need. In fact, I'd much prefer anyone able to become possessed remain outside the circle."

Vincent wanted to argue, but there was no point. Henry understood what he was about, and God knew the one thing he'd never lacked for was courage. Vincent longed to draw Henry into his arms, hold him close, and tell him he loved him. Instead, he only said, "Good luck."

"I don't need luck," Henry said, drawing on the heavy rubber glove he used for the ghost grounder. "I have science."

Henry took a deep breath and—a bit reluctantly—set aside the ghost grounder where he could easily reach it should the need arise. Every eye was on him, and he could practically taste the anticipation in the air.

After his encounter with Wellington, he was less certain than ever this was the right thing to do. He'd thought about telling Vincent and Jo about Wellington's ambitions on the way up the mountain, but they'd both been so caught up in their excitement, he'd abandoned the idea.

Vincent would surely just point out they already knew Wellington was a snake, and that alone no reason to delay their work.

For a moment, Henry wondered what might happen if he sabotaged the Electro-Séance in some small way. Just enough to prevent it from summoning the ghost.

But Jo would notice, even if Vincent didn't. She'd never forgive him.

And who knew? Perhaps she was even right. Maybe it would work, and her parents would be restored somehow. It would be the best thing for her, surely. Henry had tried his utmost, but he couldn't take the place of her actual mother or father. Surely he had to try, for her sake if nothing else.

"I'm breaking the salt line," he said aloud. He drew his boot across it, scraping a wide clear space, inviting any spirits inside. "Now the Wimshurst Machine."

There came a crack as a spark discharged, and almost everyone jumped at the loudness of the sound.

Now to invite the ghost in for supper. "William Everett," he said loudly, even as he cranked. "I call upon you to join us."

Nothing seemed to happen, and none of the mediums indicated they sensed anything. Henry's arm was beginning to tire already, and he hoped the ghost took their offering soon. "I summon the spirit of William Everett! In life you taught your young charges in this very room. As a teacher you answered the questions of your students. Now it is time to answer ours."

Nothing. Silence, save for the intermittent snap of electricity.

Then: "He's coming," Vincent said.

Within moments, a heavy tread paced slowly down the hall toward them. The small hairs stood up all over Henry's body. He continued to crank the machine to give the spirit whatever energy it needed to manifest.

Closer and closer drew the footsteps. The cool air grew intensely cold, and Henry's lungs ached with each icy breath.

Miss Blake gasped. "He's here."

"Where?" Henry asked.

"In the doorway. Looking at us." She swallowed. "I don't think he's happy to see us."

"William Everett," Lizzie said in a commanding tone. "Come into the circle and speak with us."

"He's inside the fence with you, Mr. Strauss," Miss Blake said. "Please, be careful."

Henry let go of the crank and pulled the phantom fence shut. "Jo! Connect the batteries!"

A heavy blow, seemingly from the thin air, crashed into the side of Henry's head. "Henry!" Vincent shouted.

Henry found himself blinking on the floor. He grabbed for the ghost grounder with his gloved hand—then stopped himself. It was too soon to give up. "We aren't here to fight you!" he cried.

"Spirit!" Lizzie stepped almost to the phantom fence, her skirts only inches from the electrified wires. "James Dunne Marsden was our mentor. We have come to finish his work."

Henry braced himself against another blow. But it didn't come. Instead, Miss Blake said, "That's got his attention. Mr. Strauss, try giving him a bit more from your spark machine there."

Hoping he wasn't about to gift the ghost with enough energy to seriously hurt him, Henry gave it a few more cranks.

The air before him seemed to thicken. His ears popped at the change in barometric pressure. His arm ached from landing on it on the floor, but as he continued to turn the crank, a shape began to take form.

"We have ectoplasm," he said, voice shaking from the intense cold.

The shadowy shape had once belonged to a man, though it was impossible to make out his features. There was an impression of an old-fashioned frock coat, cinched at the waist, and a tall hat.

"James," the figure whispered.

His voice was nothing human, as frightening as his appearance. It seemed to come from far away, the distance stripping it of tone and warmth, until only a sort of flat cold remained.

Lizzie put a hand to the choker she wore about her throat. "Yes. Tell us of the Grand Harmonium."

The dark mass lost some of its coherency, before re-solidifying. "I stand guard. It must be restored."

"That's what we've come to do," Vincent put in. Lizzie cast him an irritated glance, but his gaze remained on the ghost. "We have what is needed."

The cold leeched deeper into Henry's bones. Was the ghost drawing off his energy as well? "Can you please hurry?" he asked, teeth chattering.

"How did you die?" Lizzie demanded. "What happened here?"

The ghost seemed to fade slightly, like a guttering candle. "We reached for Enlightenment. But Arabella betrayed us." He began to pulse more wildly, more solid to transparent and back again. "She must be destroyed! The Grand Harmonium must be restored!"

"We will!" Vincent said. "Where is the Harmonium? Tell us!"

The shadowy figure began to lose its consistency. "The angel," he said, voice almost a whisper. "The angel will guide you."

And he was gone.

The air around Henry warmed. Vincent quickly unhooked the phantom fence and came to him. "Are you all right? He hit you rather hard."

Henry managed a smile at Vincent's concern. "Bruised, but nothing more. He does seem to be a rather violent fellow, at least in death."

Vincent's dark eyes searched his face, as if worried Henry might try to downplay an injury. Then he nodded. "Good."

"Now all we have to do is figure out what he meant," Thorpe said. "'The angel will guide you.' Do you think he means the angel statue near the entrance?"

"It's pointing downward," Jo said. Her eyes widened. "That's it. The hidden basement entrance isn't outside. It's beneath the statue itself."

# CHAPTER 13

**VINCENT STARED UP** at the statue on its plinth as they crowded into the alcove. Already, the air here felt lighter and less oppressive than it had before. He took the last cachou from his tin. A chalky residue still clung to his mouth from the teacher's ghost, but Everett seemed to have abandoned his post at the statue, at least for now.

"All right," Thorpe said. "Let's give it a push, shall we?"

Vincent leant his shoulder to the effort alongside Thorpe. The solid bulk of the marble plinth and statue failed to move an inch.

"Perhaps if we shove together?" Wellington suggested.

"They wouldn't have made it too difficult to move," Henry said. "After all, they'd want to access the basement frequently, at least while building the Harmonium. Let Jo and me take a closer look."

Vincent and Thorpe stepped back to let them through. Jo held up a lantern to illuminate the tiled floor, while Henry knelt and began to feel around the base of the statue. He ran his fingers over it methodically, until he reached some of the ornamental scrollwork at the top of the plinth. Then he paused, and a familiar smile of satisfaction curved his mouth. "Stand well back, everyone."

There came a click. The section of flooring directly in front of the statue swung open with a rusty creak of hinges.

"Brilliant, Henry," Vincent exclaimed. Henry flushed but looked pleased at the praise. "And you, too, Jo, figuring out the entrance was here to begin with."

The trapdoor opened onto utter blackness. Cold air flooded up, reeking of wet stone and rusted metal. Jo lowered the lantern into the opening. The thick shadows seemed to give way only reluctantly, revealing an iron staircase spiraling down into darkness.

"This must be it," Thorpe said. He made as though to set foot on the stairs, but Lizzie seized his arm.

"We must be sensible about this," she said. "Henry, I think your head lamps will be invaluable. And we all need to be carrying as much salt as possible."

"But the ghosts are on our side now," Miss Blake protested.

"Lizzie is right." Vincent touched the silver medallion around his neck. "Whether or not the orphanage ghosts are helping us now, Arabella is still out there. If she died here with the rest of them…"

"There's never anything good in basements," Henry murmured.

"Exactly." They shared a look of understanding. "We must be extremely cautious."

They retrieved their bags of salt from the back of the wagon, filling pockets and tying smaller bags at wrist or waist. Henry and Jo both outfitted themselves with the two miniature arc lamps, along with the heavy rucksacks carrying their batteries.

"We'll use the lanterns to begin with," Henry decided. "But the moment the flames turn blue, Jo, use your lamp. It will at least slow down any hostile spirits."

Jo nodded firmly. "I'm ready."

They returned to the trap door. "I'll go first," Vincent offered. Hopefully his clairgustance would give him advance warning if Arabella returned.

He moved slowly down the tight spiral of the staircase. It creaked and groaned, and rust flaked away with every step, but it held. "Go slow," he advised. "And not too many on the stairs at a time, just in case."

He reached the bottom safely. His lantern revealed a rough floor, raw bedrock which had been smoothed where needed to make it more or less even. As with the cliff wall above, it was dotted with tiny blue chips of crystals, glittering in the light like stars under his feet. Columns held up a thick, vaulted ceiling. The basement appeared to be a single space, stretching away all around him into empty blackness. Water dripped somewhere off in the darkness, its steady *plink* against stone likely the only sound that had disturbed the silence in years.

Henry came down after him, followed by Jo, Lizzie, Thorpe, and Miss Blake, with Wellington last. "The other ghosts have gathered around the head of the trap door," Wellington reported. "I think…this sounds mad, but I think they're afraid to follow us down."

"I don't like the sound of that," Jo said. "What could scare a ghost? They're already dead."

"Another, more powerful spirit," Lizzie said grimly.

Thorpe put a hand to her arm. "Arabella?"

"She's the one who took their lives." Vincent licked his lips, but tasted nothing. "And she's much stronger than any of them."

"But it doesn't make sense." Henry frowned as he peered at the shadows around them. "Dunne and Ortensi worked on repairing the Grand Harmonium. Arabella would have surely tried to kill both of them, if she were loose in the basement."

"Maybe." Vincent shook his head. "But she could have tried to kill Dunne at any point in the past forty years, not just here. At any rate, I don't sense anything now. Lizzie? Miss Blake, Mr. Wellington?"

"You know my talent lies elsewhere," Lizzie said. Wellington shook his head.

Miss Blake peered around, eyes narrowed. "I don't see anything. But I almost feel as though there is something? As though a presence is here, but hidden. Or hiding itself, perhaps."

"Be cautious, everyone," Henry said, which was a rather unnecessary bit of advice in Vincent's opinion. "Keep your salt at hand."

Vincent moved away from the stairs, lantern held high to cast its illumination as far as possible. Esoteric symbols were carved deep into the stone pillars, one on each of the squared-off sides.

"What are these?" Thorpe wondered.

"Sigils." Lizzie reached out and touched the nearest lightly, skimming her hand over the surface as she circled the pillar. "Life on one side, and death on the other. The remaining two sides show a bridge. Presumably one is meant to go in one direction, from life to death, and the second from death to life."

"Look," Jo called. "Is that a door?"

Vincent's heart sped up. Jo's light shone on the unfinished rock wall forming the back of the orphanage. An elaborate archway had been cut into the stone, surrounded by the same symbols as those on the pillars. Within the archway was a wooden door, banded in copper gone green with age. Had Mrs. Marsden cut deeper into the side of the mountain? Or had she fashioned the stone around a natural cave entrance?

"What's that?" Henry asked.

Vincent followed the beam of his light. A stone cylinder jutted from the floor, not far from the door. It seemed to have once had a stone cap or cover, but part of the ceiling above had collapsed onto it. Fragments of the stone cap lay scattered about, amongst the other rubble. Yet more sigils had been scratched onto the cap, but the destruction rendered it impossible to make them out.

"We must be below the chapel," Henry said, peering up at the ceiling. The space where the fallen stones had been looked like the socket of a missing tooth. "It's a wonder the floor above didn't come down also. I wouldn't advise lingering underneath it, at any rate."

"I just want to see what this is," Vincent said. He approached the cylinder cautiously. The plink of water sounded again, nearer this time, and he suddenly realized what he was looking at. Had he encountered it in a yard, he would have recognized it instantly.

The stone lip was cold and damp beneath his fingers. Vincent leaned over cautiously, holding out his lantern. It reflected in the water perhaps ten feet below.

"It's a well," he said.

The taste of river slime and wet bone flooded his mouth. The flame of his lantern faded from warm yellow, to icy blue. Before he could react, a merciless blow caught him on his shoulders. His body struck the edge of the well—then he was going up and over, tumbling into the water below.

Everything seemed to happen at once.

Vincent leaned over the well, peering inside. Miss Blake let out a warning cry—and Vincent's body jerked forward, as though pushed. He let out a short, startled shout, struck the side of the well—and vanished into it.

"Vincent!" Henry shouted, and ran toward the well.

"*Vincent...Vincent...Vincent...*" echoed back from the dark corners of the basement. But the echoes were in a woman's voice.

Arabella.

Henry's heart hammered, and sweat broke out on him despite the icy air. He peered over the edge of the well, half-expecting to be shoved in himself.

"Henry, be careful!" Jo cried.

The light of his lantern reflected off the water below—and from the thousands of crystalline inclusions in the walls of the well. The inner casing only extended a foot or so beneath the floor. The rest of the well appeared to consist of a natural channel drilled over the eons into the rock by the action of the water.

The surface rippled madly. Vincent's dark head appeared in the light of Henry's lantern, arms thrashing to keep himself afloat. Thank God.

"Vincent," Henry called down. "Are you hurt?"

The whites of Vincent's widened eyes reflected back the light. "No. But she's down here with me. Ara—"

He vanished beneath the water, as if invisible hands had shoved him under. His own hands flailed madly, trying to fight off the spirit. But of course, his attacker had no body to strike. Only implacable will.

"Vincent!" Lizzie cried, bending over the well. "We have to help him!"

"We will." Henry said. "Jo, ignite your head lamp and keep it trained down the well. And for God's sake, someone find a rope, fast!"

He tore off his own head lamp and shucked off the heavy rucksack which would drown him more surely than any ghost. His spectacles he removed and set carefully aside. Then, snatching up the copper rod of his ghost grounder, Henry scrambled over the side of the well and leapt in.

Vincent's lungs burned from lack of air, and he tore wildly at the invisible force holding him down. His hands scraped the sharp crystals jutting from the sides of the well, the icy water numbing the pain even as it leached strength from his limbs. The taste in his mouth might have either been from the ghost or from the water he'd swallowed.

Spectral hands gripped his shoulders, holding him only inches from the surface. The light of the lanterns reflected from it, taunting him with its nearness. The fingertips of one hand touched the air, but the rest of him couldn't quite reach it.

Arabella was going to drown him. He would die at her hand, as Dunne had died, as Ulysses Thorpe had likely died.

Something dark blocked the reflection of the lights on the water's surface.

A body struck the water beside him. An arm wrapped around his chest, tugging him toward the surface. But Arabella was too powerful.

This was it. He couldn't hold back a moment longer. He had to breathe—

The taste of cigars and well-done steak joined that of wet bone in his mouth.

The hands holding him under released. Vincent's head broke the surface, and he took a great, gasping breath of sweet air.

"Vincent?" Henry's voice. Henry holding him.

Because of course Henry would be the one mad enough to jump into a well with a murderous ghost.

Vincent's hair covered his eyes, so he swiped it out of the way and met Henry's gaze, wild and frantic. Their companions shouted from above, voices echoing down so they were barely intelligible.

"Dunne," Vincent croaked. "He drove her off."

But the flavor of smoke and steak were fading, in favor of slime and cold water. Frost formed along the inside of the well. The taste in Vincent's mouth strengthened. "No," he gasped. "She's too strong for him."

"Jo!" Henry yelled. "The head lamp!" He brandished the copper rod of the ghost grounder.

The bright, white light from Jo's lamp glittered on the frost, and on the crystal flakes within the rock. It was almost beautiful, or would have been if they hadn't been about to die. It reflected from the ripples of the water, and from a crystalline form just beneath...

Wait.

"Lizzie!" Vincent shouted. "Throw down salt! As much as you can! All of you!"

A rain of salt began almost instantly. Something in the well growled its fury. Henry stabbed the ghost grounder at it, though whether the rod had any effect without its connecting wire, Vincent couldn't tell.

"Don't panic," Vincent said, "but I'm going to dive under the water."

If Henry had any response, Vincent didn't hear it. The freezing water closed over his head again, but this time he directed his gaze away from the surface.

There. On a natural ledge only a few feet down, rested an object, covered in a layer of crystals precipitated out of the water. Vincent grasped it with both hands. The crystals had welded it to the ledge, but a few jerks, and it popped free.

Vincent's head broke the surface. He held his prize aloft, focusing all of his mediumistic talent on it. "Arabella! I banish you from this place! Trouble us no more."

A screech of thwarted rage sounded from just above them. A cold wind tore upward, out of the well, and the blue flames of the lanterns flickered madly.

Then silence. The air grew warmer, and the lanterns burned yellow again.

"She's gone," Miss Blake called down. "What did you do?"

Henry blinked owlishly. "I can't see without my spectacles. What the devil is that?"

"A skull," Vincent said. "Specifically, Arabella's skull." He peered up, imagined the stone cap intact and sliding over the top of the well, sealing him inside. "Unless I am very mistaken, this is where she died."

Henry crouched over one of the lanterns, his blankets spread out to trap the warmth of the flames. His clothing had at least stopped dripping, but it clung unpleasantly to his skin. If only he'd thought to bring a change from the mansion. Vincent, crouching over a lantern of his own, was in no better state.

Thorpe had returned with rope to get them out of the well, before going back to the cart again to fetch the blankets they'd used to pad the pieces of the Electro-Séance for transport. While everyone else examined the door, Henry and Vincent strove to warm themselves as best they could.

"Are you all right?" Henry asked.

They'd both been shaking with cold at first, but Vincent's tremors seemed to have stopped. His black hair was a mess, hanging limply around his face and still dripping onto the blanket. "I'm fine. Much warmer now." He paused, glancing at the others, then back at Henry. "You came in after me."

"Of course I did."

"More specifically, you leapt into a well with a ghost in the process of drowning me, with nothing more than a copper rod to save you." The corners of Vincent's mouth turned up slightly. "Not to suggest your rod isn't impressive, of course."

Henry snorted. "Villain."

"You love it."

"I do." Henry reached out a hand and caught Vincent's fingers in his. "Of course I jumped in. What else was I to do? Watch her drown you?"

"You didn't even know if it would work. You might have died."

Henry shrugged awkwardly. "You were definitely going to die if I stood there and did nothing."

Vincent let out a long sigh of breath. "I just...thank you, Henry."

"I'd do it again."

"I know." Vincent's dark eyes met his. "It's why I love you so."

Warmth rose to Henry's cheeks, and he glanced away. He wasn't particularly brave; he'd had no choice, that was all. The thought of losing Vincent had overpowered every other fear. Even now, the memory of Vincent's head vanishing beneath the water made his stomach roil with acid. "I love you, too." He nodded at the burlap sack on the floor beside them. "So, what are we going to do with this?"

While they'd set about warming themselves, Lizzie had taken the skull and packed it in salt to keep Arabella from manifesting again. Hopefully.

"I don't know. Keep it with us, for now, in case Lizzie was wrong and she's able to return despite the salt." Vincent looked in the direction of the well. "The well cap was broken in the ceiling collapse. There are sigils inscribed on the fragments, though, did you see? They must have held her in all these years."

"Which is why she didn't try to kill Dunne earlier," Henry guessed. "She was trapped here. If not for the chance fall, she might still be."

Vincent shook his head. "If the rock fall hadn't occurred...I suppose Lizzie and I would have come here with Dunne and Ortensi, assuming Ortensi ever found a suitable replacement for the Astral Key. Or if the elder Mr. Thorpe contacted us after his wife died and offered the original." He turned his face toward the darkness. "I would never have met you."

Henry shrugged. He wasn't so selfish as to suggest that would be the greater loss. "You would have found someone else."

"Someone who would jump in a well for me?" A grin curved Vincent's mouth. "Someone whose idea of pillow talk is to tell me all about electric magnetism—"

"Electro-magnetism."

"—and catheter rays—"

"Cathode rays, and you very well know it." Henry gave him a mock-glare. "If you find that romantic, I suppose I ought to tell you I have a theory."

"My heart is all a-flutter."

"Arabella is an incredibly powerful entity. I think I know why." Henry gestured vaguely at the ground beneath their feet. "We think Mrs. Marsden's spirit guide chose this place because the rock has some sort of unique properties. Clearly, judging by the skull, the water in the well has a high mineral content. I wouldn't be surprised if Marsden had the children drink from it each day."

"Probably." Vincent frowned. "I wonder if it does have any effects?

On living mediums, I mean. If we drank it, would our abilities be heightened?"

"I can't say." Henry took off his blanket, using it to blot up a few patches on his clothes that were still dripping. "However, if I am correct, the water amplified Arabella's power quite a bit after her death. The other ghosts here are unusually strong simply through proximity. Arabella drowned in the well, and her bones have been soaking in the water ever since."

"No wonder she has such strength," Vincent murmured. He rose to his feet and put out his hand to help Henry up. Henry held onto it for a few seconds longer than strictly necessary, before reluctantly letting go.

"I could be mistaken, of course," Henry said. "We would have to set up some sort of experiment to be sure."

"I think we can accept your suggestion as a working hypothesis," Vincent said wryly. "See what you've done to me? I'm using words like *hypothesis* in conversation now. Dreadful."

Henry rolled his eyes. "Very. Your poet friends would be aghast at the alteration to your character."

"I judge it to be for the good." Vincent took the sack holding the salt-packed skull and secured it to his bracers. It bumped against his hip, but was at least out of the way of his hands. "We should join the others."

# CHAPTER 14

**"ANY PROGRESS?" HENRY** asked as they approached.

"Locked," Miss Blake said. She shook the latch as if to prove her point. "We're going to have to find a hatchet to chop through it, I fear."

"Henry?" Lizzie asked. "Can you pick it?"

Before going into business with Vincent and Lizzie, Henry had owned a small repair shop. Though he wasn't a professional locksmith by any means, he'd tinkered with them enough to learn the rudiments of lock picking. The skill had come in handy more than once. "Let me examine the lock. Jo, if you'd be so good as to hold your lantern as close as you can."

He retrieved his bag from where he'd left it by the well and settled on his knees in front of the door. The latch was ornate and deeply corroded. Likely the tumblers would be stiff, if not stuck together entirely. After applying some oil, he waited a few minutes for it to do its work, then began to probe the lock.

Fortunately, for all its outward ornament, the mechanism itself was simple enough. Within a few moments, there came a click, and the latch popped open.

Henry rose to his feet and took a deep breath. A cold breeze shivered over his skin, and Miss Blake's eyes widened, even as Vincent licked his lips.

"The ghosts from the orphanage have gathered behind us," Miss

Blake reported. "Everett, the nurse, the children. Another man who might be Mr. Marsden—I wonder where he's been lurking? They're waiting for the door to open."

Wellington drew out his emerald-studded cross and pressed it to his lips, murmuring in a low voice. Thorpe glanced nervously over his shoulder, as if he thought to see the spirits himself. A charge hung in the air, crackling along even Henry's nerves. What must it feel like to the mediums?

"Are we in danger?" Thorpe asked. He took a step to the side, putting himself between Lizzie and where the ghosts presumably waited.

"We've come too far to turn back now," Wellington said. He stepped past Henry, grasped the door, and threw it open.

Vincent all but held his breath as the room beyond was revealed.

Something in the darkness flashed in the lantern light. Jo's head lamp caught another reflection, and another, and the breath stopped in Vincent's throat.

"Dear God," Henry murmured. "It's beautiful."

Too many flavors flooded Vincent's mouth for him to easily distinguish the spirits of the orphanage. But he sensed they hung back, waiting, as first Wellington, then Henry, then the rest of them moved inside.

A natural cave lay beyond the door...but what a cave it was. Every inch of the irregular walls was spangled with blue crystals, glowing and flashing. Some of the crystals were tiny, no more than the size of a thumbnail. Others reached twice the height of a man in length. They speared down from the ceiling, out from the gently curving walls. Someone had smoothed a large swath of the floor in order to comfortably walk on it, but otherwise the place had been left untouched by human hands.

"It's like standing inside a giant geode," Jo said. Her voice echoed oddly from the sharp crystals, vanishing into the darkness, then murmuring back at them, as though a thousand spirits whispered in return.

Vincent's skin prickled, as if the air were charged. A low hum vibrated in his blood, his bones, his teeth. Power, just as he'd sensed from the Astral Key. "Do you feel that?"

"Yes," Lizzie murmured. Miss Blake nodded as well.

"The crystals," Wellington said. "It must be."

"I don't feel anything," Henry said. Jo and Thorpe murmured assent.

"It must only affect those with psychical abilities."

"And spirits, I'd bet," Lizzie said. "I'm glad we have Arabella safely contained."

They moved farther into the cavern. The crystals reflected their lights, filling the cave with sparkling blue. "Look." Wellington said. "Is that…?"

"The Grand Harmonium," Henry murmured. "It must be."

In the center of the cavern stood a machine like nothing Vincent had ever seen before. There were indeed cogs and wheels, wires and Crookes tubes. But interspersed among them were more arcane parts. Jade plaques, inset with symbols Vincent didn't recognize. The skull of some animal, carved with maze-like patterns. Crystals of every description, some of them shaped and some left in their natural state. Feathers painted with strange designs.

Jo let out a gasp. "What is that?"

A figure in a white robe lay at the base of the Grand Harmonium. Its hands rested on its chest, and bare feet peeked out from beneath the long robe. Black hair streamed from its head, and a strange mask, set with some of the same crystals as the Grand Harmonium, covered the upper half of its face.

"Be careful," Miss Blake said.

Vincent swallowed and approached the shape, along with Henry and Thorpe. The figure proved to be a woman's, her flesh tinged faintly with blue. A rusty stain covered her robe over her chest. She didn't appear to be breathing.

Still, he crouched by her and stretched out a reluctant hand. His fingers pressed against her neck.

The flesh was pliable, but like ice. No pulse fluttered beneath his touch.

"She's dead," he said.

"She isn't the only one." Henry pointed to the side of the cave nearest them.

A row of bodies lay there, nearly hidden from sight by a bulge in the wall. These were far less preserved than the one in front of the Grand Harmonium. Their features were withered, lips pulled back to expose the teeth, eyes sunken into nothing, their clothing in tatters. Horribly, a fine layer of crystals seemed to have grown over their leathery skin, like a dusting of salt or pale mold. Larger crystals showed in the hollows of their eyes and gleamed within the mouths of those whose jaws gaped open.

"That's...disturbing," Vincent said, as calmly as he could.

"These must be the missing dead." Thorpe's white skin had taken on a bluish hue from the myriad reflections all around them. "Miss Gibson. William Everett. Mr. Marsden. The children."

"It must be Mrs. Marsden in front of the Harmonium." Lizzie's skirts rustled as she joined him. "Dunne and Ortensi surely laid them out, when they returned."

"But what *happened* to them?" Henry knelt by the bodies, not quite touching them. "The plaque claimed Arabella murdered them, but there aren't any obvious wounds. I'd assumed she'd used poison, but surely they would have been in the dining room if that were the case, not down here. Though I suppose Dunne and Ortensi might have moved them. And the crystals...their deposition seems unnatural. Though I'm no geologist, of course."

"Here!" Miss Blake called from the other side of the cave. "I've found something as well."

Tucked away into a hollow of the wall stood a small desk. On it was an inkwell, the ink long dried up, a pen, and a sealed box.

At the sight of the box, an odd feeling settled into Vincent's stomach, as if he'd swallowed a lead weight. Only two people had been in the cavern since the night Arabella had somehow murdered almost everyone in the orphanage. Anything in here likely belonged to either Dunne or Ortensi.

Thorpe clearly had the same idea, because he said, "Elizabeth? Perhaps you and Mr. Night should be the ones to open it."

Lizzie glanced at Vincent, her green eyes questioning. He nodded. "Go ahead."

Everyone else drew back. The box had no lock. Lizzie flipped open the latches and lifted the lid.

Papers. Papers bearing Dunne's familiar handwriting.

The answers they'd been looking for.

Lizzie carefully removed items from the box. A journal. A loose stack of pages. And lastly, what appeared to be the plans for the Grand Harmonium.

"May I see those?" Henry asked.

"Considering you and Jo are the only ones likely to understand them," Lizzie said wryly, and passed them over. Henry and Jo immediately put their heads together, murmuring and pointing.

At the bottom of the box were a number of what, at first glance, appeared to be plain white shirts. But when Lizzie drew them out, they proved to be studded with crystals and gold wire, much like the mask on Mrs. Marsden's body.

Vincent picked up the journal. Its leather binding was old and worn, and he wondered if it had been Dunne's from childhood, or was a later acquisition. He could simply open it, and yet now that the moment had come, he wasn't certain he wanted to. Once he learned the answers inside, he could never unlearn them. His view of Dunne would change, one way or another.

"What do the plans tell you?" Wellington asked. He seemed uninterested in the rest of the contents of the box, but hovered near Henry and Jo. "Can we repair the machine and make it work again?"

Henry's mouth tightened, but Jo said, "I think so. It looks like Dunne and Ortensi did most of the work already. Everything is here except for the Astral Key and the 'vestments'—oh, I think that must mean those shirts."

Miss Blake eyed the Harmonium. "How does it work, exactly?"

"It appears to function on similar principles as any séance." Henry glanced from the plans to the machine and back. "A group of people gather, holding hands while wearing the shirts. I suppose those are meant to somehow amplify their energy, or make it easier for the medium to utilize. However, where a normal séance is focused upon a single medium, the Grand Harmonium makes use of two mediums. Either end of the circle attach themselves to the machine via these wires. The two mediums place their hands on these plates, one to either side of the Astral Key."

"It looks as though the Grand Harmonium amplifies the spiritual energy of the circle." Jo pointed to some of the components, though they meant nothing to Vincent. "The mediums act as a focus for the energy, concentrating it into the Astral Key."

"And presumably the Astral Key opens a gateway to the other side, through which the spirits of the departed can be summoned back into this world," Henry finished. "Jo and I will inspect the Grand Harmonium carefully. I only wish I was familiar with all the principles at work here."

"Does anyone even know what this is?" Jo asked doubtfully, pointing at the carved skull.

The journal weighed heavy in Vincent's hands. "Perhaps there are answers here."

Henry cleared his throat. "If…if it would be easier for someone else to look over it…"

"No." Vincent sighed and straightened his back. "I'll do it."

Opening the worn cover, he began to read.

*April 30, 1858*

*Returning was harder than I ever imagined. Seeing them lying there, bodies strangely mummified by the crystals, makes our task both easier and harder. Easier, because there are vessels for them to return to once we can repair the Grand Harmonium. Harder, because they are a constant reminder of betrayal. Of guilt. Of the blood on her hands…and on mine.*

*No. I must relate these things in order. This journal is meant to become a basis for the book I shall eventually write, once everything is restored. More: it will inform all the books written after, about the most important discovery in human history. To that end, I must make a proper record.*

*My name is James Dunne Marsden, though I have as of late gone by James Dunne. My first name, before Mother remarried. With me in my endeavors is Sylvester Ortensi.*

*My mother ~~was~~ is Mrs. Betsy Marsden, perhaps the most brilliant medium and spiritualist thinker ever to have lived. Her early years were spent in upstate New York, in the heart of the so-called "Burned Over District." She discovered her mediumistic talents as a young woman, when she became deeply ill. At the height of her fever, she fell into a trance. A spirit came to her and introduced itself as Xabat. It offered to guide her development as a medium. As proof of its good intent and friendship, it healed her from her illness.*

*From then on, her talents increased. Eventually, Xabat told her it was time for her great work. Together they would change the world.*

*The spirit guided her to the cave beneath Angel Mountain and explained its many properties to her. Realizing its potential, she built Angel's Shadow Orphanage, so young mediums might not only gain proper instruction in the use of their talents, but have the growth of those talents fed by the spiritual properties of the crystals in the rock and water.*

*Shortly thereafter, Xabat revealed to her the greatest secret of all. A sort of machine, which, when properly constructed, would reverse death itself.*

*The implications were not lost on her, nor on those of her followers who worked with her at the orphanage, caring for the young mediums. Mrs. Marsden named it the Grand Harmonium, for it would unify the worlds of life and death forevermore. The veil separating us would become as permeable as the boundary between water and air, and as easy to cross.*

*Imagine, having the great thinkers of history gathered together, all debating and testing their genius together. What wonders might they create for the world? Though they would have no intact bodies to return to, Xabat assured us that with fine materials, anyone could be restored to fleshly life.*

*Imagine, young mothers never again needing to fear they will wear mourning clothes for their little ones. No more orphans, left alone in a cruel world by illness or the heavy hand of fate.*

*Truly, a new paradise awaited.*

*Xabat provided the plans for the Grand Harmonium in a series of visions. Mrs. Marsden and her followers faithfully executed these plans, and after a long period of gathering the proper materials, completed the machine. It remained only to test it. And Xabat decreed Mrs. Marsden herself would be the first trial.*

*She submitted to this command gracefully, for was it not just she should bear the risks, before wishing anyone else to do so? And indeed, all would have been well, save for one thing.*

*None of us knew. None of us even suspected.*

*I'm trying to write this narrative with the serenity of an outsider. And I know, as soon as we fix the Grand Harmonium, all will be well. All will be well.*

*I don't understand how I never saw it.*

*~~Mother~~ ~~Mrs. Marsden~~ Mother had us compete amongst ourselves. Only the strongest mediums, she said, could correctly focus the psychical energy upon the Astral Key. We all worked hard to prove ourselves, and I swear it was not favoritism that led her to choose Arabella and me. We were the best. And after she chose us, we applied ourselves twice as hard to our studies.*

*Night after night, we worked together. We were only a year apart, so we'd spent almost our entire lives in each other's company. We were as close as it was possible for siblings to be. Or so I believed.*

*I was wrong. I was so wrong.*

*Perhaps the intensity of our studies broke my sister's mind. She began to question our mother about Xabat, claiming the spirit spied on us. That she could feel it watching, when none of us sensed its presence. Even though Xabat had healed our mother from her long-ago illness, even though it had done nothing more than patiently guide and instruct us, Arabella grew afraid of it. Paranoid.*

*Perhaps an alienist might have seen the signs and recognized her growing madness. I put it down to nerves, as did everyone else. And in time, once our mother explained what was at stake yet again—that we might change the world—Arabella seemed to understand. She said she'd been wrong, that she wanted to help activate the Grand Harmonium.*

*Everything seemed to be going perfectly. We all gathered in the cave, around the Harmonium. I will admit to being afraid when Mother submitted to death. We held her down together, and her husband placed a pillow over her face. She struggled, in the end. But we had to be strong in our faith. So we kept holding her until long after she was still.*

*Seeing my mother lying there, dead at our hands, almost undid me. But I held tight to my faith in her, in Xabat, in the great work. We placed her body before the Grand Harmonium, as she had directed us to, and took our places.*

*And it worked.*

*It worked.*

*That is the thought I cling to in the long nights, when guilt and anger and fear tighten around my neck like a noose. It worked. Life returned to her. She rose, smiling, to her feet.*

*Then Arabella struck.*

*I don't know if she had planned it beforehand, or if her madness returned suddenly. The former, I suspect, because why else would she have secreted a knife on her person? She cried out and flung herself bodily on our mother and buried the knife in her heart.*

*She killed our mother for a second time in front of my eyes. And such an act would surely have been terrible enough alone. But she was a focal point for the psychical energy, and without her in place, something went wrong with the machine. Some kind of energy surge, I suppose, traveling back through the circle from Mr. Everett, who was nearest her, to Sylvester, who was closest to me.*

*Part of the machine seemed to explode, though there were no flames. Everett, Miss Gibson, Mr. Marsden, Morehouse, Brown, and Smith, fell dead at once. Green twitched and gasped before he died. Thorpe was knocked unconscious, and Sylvester left dazed. I suppose the energy must have spent itself by the time it reached Thorpe.*

*No words can adequately describe my horror. Arabella had not only murdered our mother at the very moment of our triumph, but by her actions slaughtered our stepfather, our teachers, our friends.*

*She tried to run, when she saw what she'd done. I was half out of my mind with grief, and I chased after her. We struggled outside the door, and she tried to push me away. I shoved her at the same time, and she fell backward. Into the well.*

*We'd all drunk from the well before the ritual, so the cap was off. I heard her body hit the sides, followed by a splash.*

*She cried for help. Begged me to throw down a rope. To do something to save her.*

*I did nothing. Just sat alone in the dark, paralyzed with horror.*

*I killed her. She murdered our family, our friends, and then I killed her.*

*Sylvester found me screaming and weeping by the well. I don't know how much time had passed. He held me, but we both knew what had to be done. We had no means of retrieving Arabella's body, so we put the well cap in place and inscribed symbols on it we hoped would hold in her ghost, should she fail to cross the veil.*

*Afterward, we fled. I don't know what happened to Thorpe. Everything is a blur of fear and grief and guilt.*

*I reverted to my original name of Dunne, hoping to distance myself from what had happened. Sylvester and I stayed together, using our skills as we could to survive. In time, though, when the wound was less raw, we began to speak of the Grand Harmonium.*

*The machine was damaged, but it had been built once. Surely it could be rebuilt, repaired. Some of its components would be easy to replace, and others much more difficult, especially as we didn't have Xabat's guidance. I did try to call upon the spirit, but it failed to answer me, or Sylvester. Mother always said it could only speak to certain types of minds, and I suppose ours were inadequate to the task. Perhaps Arabella had been able to half perceive it, and her twisted mind cast Xabat as a threat rather than the savior it was. Instead of crafting objects directly under its guidance, we would have to learn how to make them ourselves, or find them somewhere.*

*But we will. It may take years—decades—to obtain the knowledge ourselves. But we know the Grand Harmonium does work. It does restore the dead to life.*

*So what does it matter if we dedicate decades to the task? In the end, death itself will give way. The living and the dead will be reunited. Arabella's crime will be wiped away.*

*As will mine. The blood will be washed from our hands.*

*At present, the Grand Harmonium is in poor shape. We have reconstructed what we can. Our path ahead is clear. Sylvester will go out into the world and find substitutes for the more esoteric components. And I will find two apprentices, ones just as strong as Arabella and I were. Stronger, even.*

*Strong, but loyal. That was where things went wrong. Arabella betrayed us. My apprentices will not. I will make certain of their character. And I will wait to speak of the Grand Harmonium to them until they are standing before it at last.*

*There is too much to risk otherwise.*

# CHAPTER 15

"There's more." Vincent's fingers trembled visibly as he flipped through the journal. Henry longed to go to him, to put his hands on Vincent's and still their shaking. "Most of the following entries are about repairing the Grand Harmonium. They came here every two to three years, at first. Then the entries are farther apart." He flipped impatiently to the end. "Here. Here, Lizzie. Listen."

He cleared his throat and read: *"I have the greatest of hopes for these new apprentices. Vincent and Elizabeth soak up my teachings like sponges, desperate to know more. But it is more than that. I look at them and my heart is full, in a way it never was in my younger days. Perhaps it is because they came to me in such dire straits, I don't know. I only know I care for them. Should anything befall them, I will be devastated. As will Sylvester; he is so very fond of them as well.*

*"I have kept my vow to hold the Grand Harmonium and its workings secret, even from them. I haven't forgotten my own sister murdered our mother and betrayed the very world. I trusted Arabella above all others, so even though my judgment urges me to confide in Vincent and Elizabeth, I must hold back. Someday soon, once Sylvester finds a replacement for the Astral Key, we'll bring them here. Show them this wonder. Reveal everything.*

*"Until then...I feel almost as though, after all these years, I have a family once again."*

Silence fell after Vincent's words. Lizzie closed her eyes. Only the sound of their breathing broke the utter stillness.

Henry wanted to pull Vincent close, and hold him, and let him think or talk, or whatever he needed to do. But he couldn't, so he only said, "Vincent?"

Vincent took a shuddering breath and blinked rapidly. Lizzie pulled out a handkerchief and dabbed at her eyes. Thorpe put a hand to her arm, and she turned into him.

"I'm all right," Vincent said. *"We're* all right." His eyes shone as he met Henry's gaze. "Do you understand what this means? He never meant to betray us. He loved us. We weren't wrong about him."

Henry wanted to ask if Dunne had recorded what happened to the apprentices before them. But he hesitated, unwilling to spoil the moment.

"Now that this drama is concluded," Wellington said, spoiling it for him, "can we get to the purpose we came here for?"

Vincent nodded. Lizzie straightened and turned to him. Their eyes met, and an identical expression of determination settled over their features.

"Yes," Vincent said. "Let's fulfill Dunne's dream at last. We'll finish fixing the Grand Harmonium. Bring back his mother, then Dunne himself." He took a deep breath and let it out. "The past undone. The blood washed from our hands."

Henry and Jo set about checking over the Grand Harmonium carefully, while the mediums gathered around the journal, where they'd found a description of the needed ritual. Thorpe looked uncertainly from one group to the other, before approaching Henry and Jo. "Is there anything I can assist with?"

"We need to put the Astral Key in place, if you would be so kind as to give it to Jo," Henry said. He knelt by the Grand Harmonium, examining some of the gears. "I wish I understood its precise operation."

It was a machine of sorts, that was clear enough. But at least half of it was composed of objects with psychical or spiritual significance, but which meant nothing to him whatsoever. Ortensi had spoken of combing through the libraries of the great houses in Europe, and visiting the spirit workers of far-flung tribes. The things he had learned had allowed him to replace almost everything that had been destroyed. But as for whatever principles they worked on...Henry couldn't even begin to guess.

Vincent might, though. With enough study, at any rate. Perhaps the two of them together...

But no. There would be no together after today. If they could get the

Grand Harmonium to operate, it would resurrect Dunne, and Mrs. Marsden, and the rest of those whose bodies lay here. Perhaps even Ortensi, if they decided his crimes were justified. And from there they would fulfill the dream Dunne had written of in his journal, returning the great minds of history to life.

What place was there for Henry in such a scenario?

"It sounds like even Mrs. Marsden didn't know how it worked," Jo put in. "Since Ortensi didn't have a spirit to guide him putting it back together, he probably understood it better than anyone."

Thorpe clasped his hands behind his back, and leaned over to peer at the carved skull. "How did they gather the original materials to build the machine, I wonder? Certainly they didn't work on it for decades."

"I haven't the slightest notion." Henry tested a wire and found it secure. "Perhaps the spirit in question guided more than one medium? Unless Dunne's journal mentions it somewhere, we're unlikely to ever know."

Thorpe took the Astral Key from inside his pocket and carefully unwrapped it. "What does the Grand Harmonium *do,* though? That is, we know it brings the dead back to life. But it still needs a circle just like any séance."

Henry wished he'd learned more about the esoteric aspects of the medium's art. But he'd never had to; crystals and talking boards were Lizzie and Vincent's province. "If I had to guess, it seems as though it amplifies the energy provided by the circle, and...hmm. Attunes the Astral Key in some fashion?"

"I think you're right." Jo pointed to a cluster of gears and crystals carved with symbols. "I wonder...can the Astral Key fit many doors? And these tell it which to open?"

"So if they were changed, they would affect the door," Henry said slowly. "Tell it to open somewhere else?"

"Or which direction to swing?" Jo murmured.

"Doors to where?" Thorpe asked.

Henry took off his spectacles and wiped them carefully with his still-damp handkerchief. "I couldn't guess. And this is all wild speculation on our part, of course. Let's add the Astral Key and finish it. Jo, if you would do the honors, I'll affix it in place."

She took the flat black circle from Thorpe and set it carefully into the cradle at the center of the machine. Henry leaned in and tightened the clamps. Once it was secure, he stepped back and surveyed their work.

Some aspect of the Harmonium seemed to have shifted with the final addition. It was surely only his imagination, but he couldn't help but think the Astral Key looked like the pupil of a great eye. It made him feel watched, and he suppressed a shiver.

Thorpe seemed to share his unease, because he shifted from foot to foot, then said, "Is there any way to make the process safer? According to the journal, when Arabella left her place at the focus, it caused a—how did Dunne put it? Energy surge. Not to suggest any of us would do such a thing as she did, but mistakes do occur. Is there any way to insulate ourselves from such an event?"

"I asked myself the same thing while Jo and I went over the machine." Henry pointed to the two plates, through which the energy of the circle would enter the Grand Harmonium. "Should there be some danger, if the two people either end lift their hands at the same moment, it will stop the flow of energy in what should be a safe manner. I will stand nearest Vincent, on the left."

"I shall take the right," Thorpe offered, but Henry shook his head.

"Forgive me, Mr. Thorpe. You are a good man, but Jo's reflexes are likely quicker than yours due to her youth." Not to mention Henry trusted Jo to act sensibly in an emergency, though saying that part out loud to their employer seemed inadvisable. "I would prefer to have her in such a critical position. If you don't have any objections, Jo?"

She nodded firmly. "I won't let you down, Henry."

"I know it." He put a hand to her shoulder.

Thorpe wandered off. Henry stared at the Grand Harmonium, wishing he understood more about it. At least its operation had already been proven, when Mrs. Marsden had been restored the first time, all those years ago. Though it didn't sound as though there had been much time between her revival and Arabella's murderous act, it still soothed some of the apprehensions Henry would have ordinarily entertained about using such a mysterious device.

Not to mention… "I can't believe I'm going to see Mama and Daddy again," Jo said in a low voice. Tears swam in her big eyes. "This really is going to change everything, isn't it, Henry?"

"It is." Ordinarily, he'd be the first to rejoice in such changes. To imagine what they might have to offer to the rest of the world.

But all he could see was the ending of the little family he'd built.

With Dunne alive again, Vincent and Lizzie would return to their life with him. Now that they knew the truth, knew he had indeed cared for them, there was no reason to remain apart. And of course Jo would return to her old life with her parents; it was only natural.

Henry had only ever been a way station for them. Certainly he wasn't selfish enough to begrudge them the happiness the Grand Harmonium would restore. Jo most of all; he couldn't wait to see the joy in her eyes when her mother and father embraced her anew.

But he could already sense how lonely his life would be without any of them. Should he close the shop? What did Thorpe intend to do with the Grand Harmonium in the longer term? Perhaps he would need someone to help keep it running. Henry might find a place here…except Wellington would be here as well.

Whatever happened, he would have to warn Thorpe against Wellington before they parted. Wellington clearly meant to make his fortune from the Grand Harmonium, and if Thorpe didn't go along with his plans, Wellington wouldn't hesitate to betray him in some fashion.

For now, though, Wellington needed the machine operational and its rightful owner pleased with its operation. That should keep him in line for a time.

Jo's hand found his, interrupting his brooding thoughts. "Are you looking forward to seeing your parents again?"

Henry let out a long breath. "Mother is at peace. The world treated her cruelly the last few years of her life, and I'm not certain it would be right to bring her back. If I received some signal indicating she truly wishes to return, my stance would change, naturally."

"I'm sure my parents will have news of her, and the rest of the family beyond the veil," she said. "You can just ask them."

"I will."

"And your father?" She hesitated. "What if…what if he comes back and doesn't want a colored niece, any more than he did before he died?"

"I pray death grants a perspective beyond life. A wisdom beyond what we have here. But if not…" He trailed off and turned to her. Putting both hands on her shoulders, he leaned over slightly so as to look her level in the eye. "I will always choose you, Jo. Always. Nothing will ever change that."

She blinked rapidly, then threw her arms around him. As he hugged her back, Wellington cleared his throat. "I believe the mediums are ready to start."

Henry ground his teeth together. Of course Wellington would ruin his chance to say goodbye to the girl who was the closest thing he would ever have to a child. Jo let go of him and stepped back, wiping hastily at her eyes. "We're ready," she said.

Henry glanced at Vincent, expecting to find sympathy in his lover's dark gaze. But Vincent was focused entirely on the Grand Harmonium, and didn't spare him so much as a glance. "Good," Vincent said. "Let's begin."

Vincent stood impatiently by the machine, while those who would form the circle pulled on the shirts that would help harness their energy. "We'll resurrect Mrs. Marsden first," he said. "She knows more than any of us about the operation of the Harmonium."

"And about these 'fine materials.'" Henry's voice was muffled by the shirt he currently pulled over his head. Fortunately they were loose enough to fit over the clothing of everyone who would form the circle. His face popped out the neck hole, and he added, "If we need to gather some sort of ingredients, for example."

Vincent felt as though his skin were electrified, little prickles that made him restless. "It had best not be anything too onerous."

"If it is, then it is." Lizzie watched him from beneath her lids. "I know you want to see Dunne again, but you *cannot* rush through this ritual, Vincent. Or through anything Mrs. Marsden requires of us after. We've already seen the consequences of a mistake, and they aren't pretty." She pointed at the bodies so carefully arranged behind her.

Lizzie didn't—couldn't—understand. She never had, because she didn't bear the same weight of guilt as Vincent. Ever since the moment he'd opened his eyes and found Dunne dead on the floor beside him, something seemed to lay atop his heart, pressing down, keeping it from expanding in a full beat.

This was his chance to remove the weight.

Still, she was right. Bad enough his hands had killed Dunne the first time. At least then they'd been under Arabella's control. If something went wrong now, there was no one to blame but Vincent himself.

He could sense Dunne now, the taste of cigars and steak in his mouth, even through the confusion of the other spirits present. All of them waiting for him to act, to restore them to life.

He gave Lizzie a nod and closed his eyes, concentrating on his breathing, using the techniques Dunne had taught him so long ago. By the time those forming the circle had shuffled into place, his heart beat had slowed, and he felt centered again.

Vincent placed one hand on the mechanism holding the Astral Key in place, and the other on the metal plate in front of him. Lizzie mirrored his stance. "Those of you in the circle," he said, "take each other's hands. Henry, Jo, place your free hand on the nearest metal plate. Now, all of you, concentrate on the flow of energy. Of passing it one to the next, and into the Grand Harmonium."

"Do we need to put out the lanterns?" Jo asked.

A normal séance would be conducted in near darkness. But of course, this was no normal séance. Nor was it a normal place. There was an energy here, buzzing in Vincent's bones, in the space behind his eyes. The crystals flashed and gleamed, and the metal plate beneath his fingers warmed to the heat of his body.

"No. It isn't strong enough to interfere with the working of the machine." It wasn't even strong enough to hold back any spirits.

The taste of fine cigars and steak was a reassurance on his tongue. They were doing the right thing. After over a year of uncertainty, they were finally on the proper path.

"Remember," he said, "whatever else happens, do not break the circle." He took a deep breath. "Lizzie? Are you ready?"

She nodded. "Let's begin."

The papers from the box included a sort of litany, or chant, to be read by the two foci. Vincent directed his concentration onto the Astral Key. "The way is open," he said.

"Open is the way," Lizzie replied.

The gears of the machine began to turn, in response to the energy gathered from the circle. The Crookes tubes shed their violet light, which blended strangely with the blue glow of the crystals. Lightning danced through the inlay on the jade plaques, and the skull rattled, the maze-like carvings filling with light as though it were a liquid poured from a bottle. Then the light reached the plates on which Vincent's and Lizzie's hands rested.

The energy slipped into Vincent like a needle into a vein. He gasped in shock, head arching. Some of his senses sharpened, while others fell away. His skin vibrated, every hair standing on end. The Astral Key began to turn sluggishly in its setting, reddish light playing across its surface.

"The way is found," he said, and tasted smoke and ash.

"We have found the way," Lizzie replied.

The light flickered, shifted hue, failing to settle on a single color.

They weren't focusing hard enough. Vincent narrowed his concentration to a fine point. He threw all of his strength, all of his will, into an effort that went beyond mental into the spiritual. The world peeled away; there was nothing but the Astral Key and the energy burning through his body. Distantly he sensed Lizzie doing the same.

"The way is open," he said through gritted teeth.

"Open is the way."

The shifting colors settled. Condensed into a hue of violet just on the edge of sight.

There.

"Open the gate," Vincent said, and Lizzie spoke with him this time in perfect harmony. "Open the gate; open the gate. Betsy Marsden, we bid you come through!"

He sensed something *click,* as though a door in the world itself had come unlatched.

The body before them took a great gasp of breath.

# CHAPTER 16

"**CLOSE THE GATE** again!" Henry shouted. "Close it!"

Sweat ran down Vincent and Lizzie's faces, and a handful of the tiny blood vessels had burst in their eyes. They looked as though they'd struggled through some great battle, or wrestled an incomprehensible weight into place.

No wonder Dunne had been looking for apprentices strong enough to endure whatever the spirit world had to throw at them.

"Let the gate be closed," they said together. "Let the gate be closed and the way sealed again."

The strange almost-light from the Astral Key faded. The buzzing filling Henry's ears from the moment the séance had begun died away. The gears slowed and stopped.

As soon as he was certain it was safe, Henry let go of Miss Blake's hand and the metal plate. Thorpe dropped to his knees beside Mrs. Marsden and put his fingers to her throat. "She has a pulse," he said in wonder.

Her eyes opened.

Thorpe jerked back. Mrs. Marsden sat up, not even needing their aid. As though her body had simply slept for an hour, rather than lying dead and cold on the ground for decades.

Henry's breath caught in his chest. A part of him hadn't truly believed it possible for the dead to return to life. And yet here was proof, before him.

How much of human striving had been for this very goal? To turn death from a bitter sting to a mere inconvenience.

He couldn't begin to imagine the ultimate implications. Once word got out, once the great minds of history were able to directly commune with those of this age, would even more miracles follow? Did they at this moment stand on the precipice of titanic change such as the world had never before known?

This was far too important for any mistakes to be made. Henry went to Mrs. Marsden and crouched at her side.

The papers on the desk went cascading to the ground, as though an invisible hand had shoved them off.

Henry flinched at the sound. Wellington clutched his gold cross and muttered something, an oddly vexed look on his face. Nothing further happened, and Henry turned his attention back to the woman watching him bemusedly. "Tell us your name."

She took off her mask, revealing ordinary features. Henry wasn't certain what he had expected, but this woman, who had returned from the far reaches of death, could have been any matron on the street. "Mrs. Betsy Marsden. But you already knew it, didn't you..." She cocked her head as if recalling some half-remembered fact. "Mr. Strauss."

His breath clogged in his throat. "How do you know my name?"

"Nothing remains hidden, once we pass beyond the veil." She offered him a beneficent smile. "Thank you for returning me to my body." She gazed around slowly. "Much time has passed on this side, I take it."

Lizzie and Vincent exchanged looks. "One could say that," Lizzie said at last.

"Your son is dead," Vincent blurted.

"Vincent!" Lizzie shot him a glare.

Henry watched Mrs. Marsden for any signs of shock, but her smile remained steady. "Of course. Did you imagine I wouldn't know?" She held out a hand to Henry. "Will you help me up, Mr. Strauss?"

"Perhaps you should take things easy," Henry said uncertainly. "You have been, er, incapacitated for some time."

She patted him on the hand. Her fingers were as warm as those of any living woman. "Not at all. One of the properties of the Grand Harmonium is to restore and rejuvenate the flesh as well as the spirit." She touched the ragged hole in her shift, where Arabella's knife must have pierced her heart. Any trace of the wound on her skin had vanished.

All the promises of the Grand Harmonium seemed to be true. Jo and Thorpe appeared awed, and Lizzie relieved. Wellington's eyes gleamed, and a small, avaricious smile played around his lips. Miss Blake stared at the risen Mrs. Marsden avidly.

Vincent reached down to help Mrs. Marsden to her feet. "We'll restore your son. Tell us what we need to do."

Henry frowned. "Using the Grand Harmonium was clearly hard on you and Lizzie. Perhaps we should go back to the mansion and allow you to rest first."

Vincent tossed his hair back from his eyes. "Surely, Henry, you've learned by now stamina is one of my greatest attributes."

Henry blushed, but Lizzie said, "This isn't a joking matter, Vincent."

"I agree." Vincent turned to Mrs. Marsden. "No doubt you spoke with your son beyond the veil and can sense his presence in this very room now. I was possessed by Ara—by a spirit," Vincent corrected. Perhaps he thought it gauche to accuse Mrs. Marsden's daughter to her face. "She used my hands to kill Dunne—James. He was our mentor, and I daresay he meant as much to Lizzie and me as your parents did to you." Vincent gestured vaguely to the fallen papers. "Dunne's notes say 'fine materials' can be used to rebuild a body for the departed. Tell us what those are, so we can bring them here and return him to life. I assume you collected them before your undertaking, and they're stored somewhere in the orphanage?"

Mrs. Marsden stared at him thoughtfully for a long moment. "I can tell you miss my son desperately. And no doubt there are others eager for reunions of their own." She glanced around the room. Jo nodded vigorously, and Thorpe inclined his chin gravely. "Well. I feel this will work even better than I initially believed it would. Let us proceed." She picked up the mask and held it in her hands. "Take your places and open the gateway."

"What of the materials?" Henry asked, surprised.

"We already have all we need here." Mrs. Marsden offered him again her beatific smile. "The Grand Harmonium shall provide, Mr. Strauss."

It didn't seem possible. Surely a body couldn't be created from thin air and wishful thinking. Henry started to say as much, then caught himself. Was he really about to argue with a woman who had been dead for forty years? Whose body had been preserved far better than it should have, who had lain cold and lifeless before him not half an hour before?

She had built the Grand Harmonium under the auspices of her spirit guide, Xabat. Together, they had engineered a machine to create miracles.

What had Henry done that was in anyway comparable? Who was he to question?

His shoulders slumped just a fraction. "Of course." He wanted to suggest Vincent and Lizzie at least rest a bit longer, even if they didn't return to the mansion, but the eager light in their eyes stopped the words in his throat. They wouldn't tolerate a delay. Not when the reunion they'd longed for was so close.

So he remained silent as they returned to the previous positions around the machine. Mrs. Marsden stood in the same spot where her body had lain, her white shift all but glowing in the refracted light from the crystals. Henry straightened his heavy, crystal-studded shirt, then took Miss Blake's hand. His other he lay on the metal plate.

Vincent and Lizzie began to chant again. Henry tried to clear his mind of worry and focus his energy on the Harmonium. A little crackle jumped between palm and metal plate, and soon *something* flowed through him. Not quite an electric charge, but close enough for the hairs on his arms to prickle. Miss Blake's hand was hot in his, and Vincent and Lizzie's jaws grew clenched. The Harmonium returned to life, and the desire to more closely inspect it while in operation prodded at Henry. He ignored it, returning his concentration to the task at hand. The quicker this was finished, the quicker Vincent and Lizzie could rest.

Unless Thorpe and Jo demanded to have their own dead returned immediately. Henry would have to put his foot down, if they did. Tomorrow would have to be soon enough. No sense risking the only two mediums they had strong enough to act as the foci.

Damn it, his concentration had lapsed again. Henry took a deep breath and bent all his will to adding his energy to the circle, letting it be drawn from them through his hand.

The Astral Key flashed once again, barely-visible light playing over it.

"It is done," Mrs. Marsden said. "The gateway is open." She held up the mask. "Now, Mr. Night, I will place this on your face."

Vincent's concentration wavered, but it seemed not to matter now that the Astral Key had been activated. "The mask?"

"Yes." She smiled. "You are indeed fine materials. Your body will hold James's spirit more than adequately. Alas, the process will remove yours in exchange."

Vincent's tongue felt thick. He didn't dare move from his place at the Grand Harmonium, lest he cause the same sort of backlash which had killed the original inhabitants of the orphanage. "Exchange?"

"Of course, child." Her voice was gentle. Sad. "Something cannot come from nothing. There is always a cost. The universe has a balance, you see." She gestured with the hand not holding the mask, turning it first palm up, then palm down. "Night and day. Life and death. Sin and redemption."

"It doesn't seem to me as though you've paid such a cost," Lizzie said. She sounded horrified, but Vincent didn't look at her, transfixed by Mrs. Marsden.

"I had a body to return to," she replied. "Preserved by the properties of the cave and the design of the spirits. My dear James has no such vessel awaiting. Surely it is only right for his slayer to provide one?"

The words sunk like hooks into his heart. Of course. What a fool he'd been.

He'd let himself imagine there would be no consequences. That the world would bend itself to allow him to walk away, guilt absolved. Return to Baltimore with Henry, happy and content knowing Dunne was once again alive. Sleep without nightmares.

The burden of his guilt lifted.

But the universe didn't work that way. He should have known it— he *did* know it. But, for a moment, he'd let himself believe.

"I understand," he said. He didn't dare look at Henry, for fear his resolve would crack. "Put the mask on me. Let Dunne take my place in this world."

"Jo!" Henry barked. "Three, two, one!"

The energy boiling through the Grand Harmonium and into Vincent abruptly ceased. Lizzie let out a startled cry. The Astral Key continued to put out its strange glow, but Vincent didn't have time to worry about why. Instead he turned and saw Henry and Jo had both lifted their hands from the metal plates.

"You could have killed us, Strauss!" Wellington exclaimed in horror.

"Don't be an idiot," Henry snapped. "And that goes double for you, Vincent!"

Of course Henry would argue. "It isn't your decision."

Henry's blue eyes widened behind the shield of glass lenses. "You can't mean to give up your body—your *life*—so Dunne can return."

Vincent drew a deep breath. The moment felt inevitable, as if he'd been on this course from the morning he'd waked to find Dunne dead, the marks of Vincent's hands around his throat. "I can and I do."

"No." Lizzie stepped away from her post at the machine. "Vincent, think. Dunne wouldn't want you to do this."

"Of course he would!" Vincent's nails bit into his palms. "He's here, in this very room, with us. If he didn't want to return, he'd just...just leave. Pass on. Not crowd ever closer."

"Even if you're right, it's no reason for you to comply," Henry argued.

Thorpe held up a hand. "Am I understanding this correctly?" His handsome face had taken on an ashen hue. "If I am to return one of my parents to life, I have to die?"

"Not you," Mrs. Marsden said. "Someone. A fresh corpse would do, could you find one. Or someone else might volunteer to make the exchange."

Thorpe shook his head rapidly. "No." He backed away from the machine. "This is horrible. I can't believe you built this abomination."

"Don't be so hasty," Wellington said. He seized Thorpe's wrist. "You're letting fear cloud your judgment."

"I miss my parents," Jo said. Tears filled her eyes and ran unheeded over her brown cheeks. "More than I can say. But they wouldn't want someone else killed just so they could live."

Henry cast her a stricken glance. She caught it and shook her head. "Don't even say it, Henry. Don't even *think* it."

It gave Vincent the opening he needed. "Do you see, Henry?" He gestured to Jo. "This is voluntary. I'm offering."

"It doesn't matter." Lizzie folded her arms. "I refuse to be a part of this travesty."

"And there is your mistake." Mrs. Marsden glided closer to Vincent, the mask with its strange crystals and jewels in her hands. "You have no say in this. The gate is already open. All that is needed is for Vincent to place the mask on his face and invite my son's spirit in."

Henry's heart raced, beating so frantically against his ribs he could barely catch his breath. "Vincent, no."

Mrs. Marsden held out the mask, and Vincent took it from her. His brown fingers traced the gold inlay, the multi-colored crystals.

"Stop!" Lizzie took a step toward them. "Vincent, I won't let you!"

He shook his head. "It isn't your choice, Lizzie. I'm sorry. Tell Dunne...just tell him I never meant for it to be like this."

Henry lunged forward and seized Vincent's wrist. Vincent tried to pull away with a snarl, but Henry clung tight. "You can't do this!"

"Don't you understand? I have to!" Vincent swallowed, throat working. "It's about balance, just as Mrs. Marsden said. About justice."

"This isn't justice!" Henry's voice broke. "His death was Arabella's fault. She stabbed their mother, but Dunne let her drown in the well while he listened. Her blood was on his hands, and she came for revenge, and I'm sorry you ended up between them. But you have to let go of this guilt. You have to see none of this was your fault. You aren't responsible for something that happened before you were even born."

"Henry's right," Lizzie said. "You know he is."

Vincent's lips parted slightly. He didn't want to put on the mask, Henry realized. He felt he should…but he didn't want to.

Mrs. Marsden's eyes narrowed and she glared at Henry. "You are interfering in things that are none of your business." Turning to Vincent, she said, "Put on the mask, child. Your end will be painless. *His* wasn't painless though, was it?"

Vincent gasped as though she'd slapped him. "What is wrong with you?" Lizzie demanded of Mrs. Marsden. "Stop saying these things!"

"Why should I?" A sneer of contempt crossed Marsden's face. "I have seen into your souls, and what did I find? Nothing but corruption. Greed. Lust. Betrayal." She shook her head. "Look into yourself, Vincent Night. You make your living on a web of lies, playacting for your clients so they will find you acceptable enough to pay. Fear and doubt poison your spirit; weakness riddles your heart. You even doubted James, the man who took you in from the streets. Left to your own devices, yours would have been a wasted life. You were nothing until he made something of you. You owe him everything."

"To hell with that," Henry snarled. He didn't know what had gone wrong, why Mrs. Marsden's demeanor had changed from warm to judgmental, and at the moment he didn't care.

Thorpe seemed to feel the same. "Now see here," he began sternly.

Mrs. Marsden turned on him. "Oh, I have, Charles. Your father needed you, and what did you do? Abandoned him. Left him to die alone, while you drank and fornicated."

Thorpe went pale. Marsden put her back to him, as though he weren't worth her time. "Put the mask on, Vincent. You have been seen and judged undeserving. Beyond redemption. The world needs James. It does not need you."

"But I do." Henry's throat constricted, fear choking his words. His fingers tightened on Vincent's wrist, hard enough to bruise. "I need you, Vincent."

Vincent's dark eyes met his, filled with grief and guilt and pain. "The world..."

"Hang the world." Barely daring to breathe, Henry touched the fingers of his free hand to Vincent's cheek. "You're my world, don't you see? I know I'm not perfect, I know you could do better, but the truth is I need you."

"So do I," Jo said in a small voice. "Vincent, please, don't leave us."

"I knew Dunne as well as you did," Lizzie said. "And I tell you now, he was not worth this. And if he were any kind of man at all, anything like the man we thought we knew, he wouldn't accept this trade. You know I'm speaking the truth."

The mask fell from Vincent's fingers.

Henry swept him into his arms, holding him close. Breathing in the citrus and musk of his scent. "I love you," he whispered fiercely. "Don't leave me. Please, don't ever leave me."

Vincent hugged him back. "I won't, Henry. I won't. I'm not...I'm not even sure what I was thinking."

"The Grand Harmonium is an abomination." Thorpe's voice shook on the words, but a look of determination was stamped on his face. "I'm sorry, Mrs. Marsden, but what you have created here is horror." Thorpe took a step toward the machine. "It must be destroyed."

There came the click of a gun cocking. "I don't think so," Miss Blake said. In her hand she held a pistol, now leveled coolly at Thorpe's head. "We've come too far to turn back. Now step away from the Grand Harmonium, or your corpse will join the others on the floor."

# CHAPTER 17

**VINCENT FELT AS** though he woke from a dream into a nightmare.

He'd already been reeling from the revelation that the Grand Harmonium couldn't restore the dead to the world of the living without taking a life in return. Dunne surely hadn't known; both he and Ortensi had written as though the Harmonium would work miracles. They'd seen only Mrs. Marsden die and live again. Seen her body mysteriously untouched by rot through all the decades after Arabella struck her down a second time.

Then Mrs. Marsden had looked at him, held out the mask, and…

And every doubt he'd had, every fear, every feeling of unworthiness had multiplied in his mind until his soul bowed beneath the weight. Her dark eyes had seemed to bore into him, peeling back his skin, until every imperfection was laid bare. He'd been judged and found lacking. Surely the world would be a better place with Dunne in it instead of him.

The voices of the ones he loved most had been the only clear thing amidst the clinging sadness. He didn't want to leave Henry. Or Jo. Or Lizzie.

Three lifelines, cast into a sea of despair.

His head cleared.

And now Miss Blake was pointing a gun at Thorpe.

Lizzie let out a hiss of rage. "What is the meaning of this?" she demanded of Miss Blake. "Put that away at once!"

"I don't think so." Miss Blake's face was pale, but her hand remained steady. "All of you, back away from the machine."

They did so, moving slowly. All except for Mrs. Marsden...and Wellington.

"I assumed if anyone betrayed us, it would be you," Vincent said to him. "But I never imagined Miss Blake would be stupid enough to work with you."

Wellington sighed. "We aren't betraying anyone. Merely preventing Mr. Thorpe from making a grievous mistake. Charles, you've let emotion blind you to the Grand Harmonium's potential."

Thorpe narrowed his eyes. "Potential? Is that what you call it?"

"It is." Wellington turned his attention to Henry. "Henry, you're a practical man. It's why we brought you here to begin with."

Henry's skin had gone white as chalk. "Brought me here?"

"Indeed. Night and Devereaux were a bonus, but there are other mediums strong enough to act as the foci. There aren't many people with enough understanding to not only complete the repairs on the Grand Harmonium, however, but to build more."

The taste of cigars flooded Vincent's mouth, overwhelming all other flavors. Something cold as ice touched the skin of his face, his left ear.

"Build more?" Henry asked.

Miss Blake's eyes glittered. "There are other places in the world similar to this, where crystal caves produce just the right conditions to allow the Harmonium to operate. Xabat has told me of them."

"Mrs. Marsden's spirit guide?" Lizzie shot a quick look at the woman in question, who stood watching them all with a slight smile playing around her lips. As if their confusion and fear pleased her.

Maybe Arabella's paranoia had been justified after all.

"The cross," a voice whispered into Vincent's ear. The voice of the dead. "Take it from him."

Vincent gave a tiny nod, imperceptible to anyone not looking directly at him. The cold vanished, the taste receding.

"Xabat could not speak to those faithful who survived the first trial. It takes a certain kind of mind to hear his call." Miss Blake smiled proudly. "The sort I have. He spoke to me of the Harmonium. Led me to the Astral Key—or rather, to the man who had it. Mr. Thorpe had already consulted with Mr. Wellington. I saw right away Mr. Wellington was...well, a practical sort of man himself."

"Once I learned the truth," Wellington said, "I knew just who we needed. I've seen your name in the journals, Henry, and heard it from the lips of mediums who fear the change you represent. Miss Blake pretended to have received spiritual guidance to enquire in the Baltimore journals, and here we all are."

Thorpe swayed slightly. Lizzie took his hand for comfort. "Blackguards, all of you," she said.

Henry's eyes narrowed behind his spectacles. He'd shoved Jo protectively behind him, and stood with his shoulders back, arms slightly out to either side. "What do you want from me?"

"Don't sound so dramatic. We're giving you an opportunity." Wellington gestured to the Grand Harmonium. "Imagine the possibilities, Henry. Not some foolish claptrap about inviting the great minds of history to join together, but real, practical uses. How much do you think a Vanderbilt or Carnegie would pay to be liberated from a body failing from age or disease, and reborn in another, young and strong?"

Vincent felt as though he'd swallowed a chunk of ice too large to melt, sitting in his belly and radiating cold. God. He'd never considered the Grand Harmonium might be used for such a purpose. No wonder Dunne and Ortensi had kept the secret close for all those years.

He expected Mrs. Marsden to speak up. To deny the corruption of her work. But she merely stood off to the side, an observer. Smiling.

Something was very wrong.

"Someone else would have to die for that to happen," Henry said.

"And their families would be well compensated. We aren't monsters, you know." Wellington spread his hands apart. "Merely…businessmen."

"So what will it be, Strauss?" Miss Blake demanded. "You'd be set for a lifetime. All you would have to do would be to maintain the Grand Harmonium and help us construct additional ones. I'm sure there are plenty of European nobility who would pay well for the chance at immortality."

"What about everyone else?" Henry's voice trembled only slightly. "If I agree to join you, will you let them go unharmed?"

"Don't trust them, Henry," Lizzie said. "They'll never let us go."

Miss Blake swung her gun around. "I think you need to—"

An unseen force wrenched her arm down and to the side. The gun went off, striking one of the crystals and sending blue chips flying into the air.

"Stop!" Wellington shouted, and drew out the gold cross.

Vincent sprang at him. Before Wellington could react, he seized him by the wrist with one hand, using the other to try and pry the cross free. For a moment, they struggled—then Vincent brought up his knee and caught Wellington a solid blow straight to the groin.

The cross fell from Wellington's grasp. It struck the floor at Vincent's feet and broke into two pieces.

No. Not broken. It had separated, rather, as though it had deliberately been fashioned to come apart. Set within the body of the cross had been an emerald stick pin, which now lay to one side.

Thorpe and Lizzie had both leapt at Miss Blake, and now wrestled her for the gun. Thorpe tore it free and pointed it at her. "Enough," he said. "Both of you, step back and keep your hands where I can see them."

Henry's eyes locked on the stick pin lying on the ground. The last of the color drained from his already pallid face. "It...it's my father's stick pin. The one he apported into my room, after he died."

The one Wellington had stolen.

The pin was surely valuable...but rather than sell it, Wellington had the cross specially made to conceal it. Which meant its value to him wasn't in the emerald and gold, but rather in the fact it had a strong bond to a spirit. It had even already been touched by Alfred Strauss's ghostly energy.

Holding a stick pin and whispering commands into it would have been noticeable. But pretending to pray before using his so-called mediumistic gifts wouldn't be particularly remarkable at all.

Except Wellington had no gifts. He'd been using the pin as a necromantic talisman to command the ghost of Henry's father.

The ghost Vincent had sensed time and again had never been Dunne. Only Alfred, fighting against the compulsions Wellington bound him with. Striving to keep his son safe.

Vincent bent down to pick up the pin. It truly was a handsome specimen, the emerald a deep, rich green, the gold finely shaped. No wonder it had held such importance for Henry's father, enough for him to apport it from his grave to his son's room, seeking to ease Henry's grief.

His fingers closed on the stick pin—and a spark seemed to leap from it, to him. A whisper in his mind, frantic and urgent, though he couldn't make out the words. Desperation and panic, and an overwhelming fear greater than any Wellington had caused.

Mrs. Marsden was still smiling.

Vincent fastened his hand around the silver talisman at his throat and pulled it off.

And Alfred flooded in.

~ * ~

Henry watched in horror as Vincent's entire body jerked. His eyes rolled back in his head, leaving only the whites visible. His hand clamped around the stick pin, knuckles going pale.

"He's being possessed!" Lizzie exclaimed.

Vincent stumbled to his feet. His sightless eyes turned toward Henry —and he lunged.

Henry tried to jerk back, expecting hands to close tight around his throat at any moment. But whatever was inside Vincent's body instead gripped Henry's shoulder with his free hand.

"It isn't her!" His voice rasped coming out, and the cadence sounded unlike Vincent...but much like a voice Henry hadn't heard in many a year. "Mrs. Marsden—whatever came back, it isn't human! Run!"

Henry's lips parted. "F-Father?"

"What a troublesome little ghost." Mrs. Marsden knelt to pick up the mask. "This has been far more entertaining than I expected. Greed, jealousy, despair, anger...what a feast you have provided. Just the thing I needed after so long a span of deprivation."

The hair on Henry's neck stood up. Lizzie took a wary step back, away from Mrs. Marsden. "What are you?"

Thorpe shifted the gun's aim from Miss Blake to Mrs. Marsden. "Answer her."

"Gladly." Her mouth widened into a grin—and kept widening, far past anything that should have been possible for human flesh. "Mrs. Marsden—the real Mrs. Marsden—knew me as Xabat." She held out a hand to Miss Blake, who came to her, eyes bright with devotion. "Betsy was a simpering fool, but perfect for my needs." Xabat cocked its head, vertebrae cracking audibly. "I spoke to her, year after year. Convinced her I was her friend. All so I could have...this." It held out an arm, as if admiring the stolen flesh. Then its smile collapsed, the change so fast it was nearly disorienting. "My plan was on the cusp of fruition, when her accursed daughter interfered. Arabella was sensitive to my energies. She saw me watching, manipulating, and grew afraid. I convinced her mother the girl suffered from overwork, but had I known what Arabella would do, I would have had her locked away in a madhouse. But now I have a second chance."

Her—its—gaze cut to Vincent. "I would have put another of my kind in his skin. But the rest of you interfered. Refused to go along with my followers' plans." It let out a heavy sigh. "I suppose I'll just have to kill you."

Xabat held up the mask. There came a rush of cold air, as though every ghost in the orphanage stampeded past in obedience to its command. A horrible creaking sounded from their withered bodies. The crystals grown over desiccated skin flashed, and a gust of putrid air poured forth.

What the devil?

Henry started to take a step closer, but at that moment, Vincent stumbled and blinked. When he looked up, his eyes were his own again.

"She's forcing the dead into their old bodies, using the power of the cavern," he gasped. "We have to get out of here."

The creaking and cracking grew louder. A leathery arm raised up, jerky as a marionette on a string. More movement came, the corpses heaving themselves to their feet. Crystals jutted from empty sockets, and teeth covered only by rags of flesh gnashed. Joints bent impossibly, in a way nothing living could endure.

Horror surged through Henry, sealing his feet to the ground. He could only stare as the first revenants made it to their feet. Then those glowing eyes found him, and the dead began to shuffle forward.

Thorpe fired the gun, painfully loud in the cavern. Everett's reanimated corpse jerked, but kept coming.

"Salt!" Lizzie shouted, and flung a handful at the nearest revenant. But the spirit was protected by a shell of flesh, and nothing happened.

"Run!" Vincent's hand yanked on Henry's arm. "Run, Henry! Everyone, run!"

The paralysis broke. Henry grabbed Vincent's hand, turned, and ran.

Vincent raced across the cavern toward the door, all but dragging Henry behind him. The taste of rancid flesh filled his mouth, gagging him to the point he couldn't sense anything else, not even Alfred Strauss.

Possession normally left the medium weak, but thankfully something about the way the cave gave energy to ghosts and mediums alike had counteracted the effect this time. He glanced over his shoulder, saw Xabat standing before the Grand Harmonium, its true nature hidden beneath Mrs. Marsden's flesh.

He'd seen it, when Alfred possessed him. Not with his eyes, but with the senses of a ghost.

A dark force occupied Mrs. Marsden's corpse, a thing of shadow and hate. Of a dozen mouths, all hungry, and a hundred eyes, all searching for prey. It fed on despair and pain, on greed and envy. No wonder he'd felt so strange, when it had tried to convince him to offer up his body to the

Grand Harmonium.

If he'd given in...it wouldn't have been Dunne who walked away in his flesh. It would have been something far more terrible.

Jo and Lizzie ran ahead of everyone else, followed by Thorpe, then Vincent and Henry. As they approached the ponderous door, it began to swing slowly shut, even though no hand touched it.

"No!" Jo shouted, and the fear in her voice wrung Vincent's heart.

The door slowed in its arc, as though something else strove to hold it open. Alfred?

Thorpe lunged past Lizzie and into the gap. The door thudded against him, though at least the counteracting force kept it from striking him hard enough to cause injury. Thorpe braced himself between the frame and the door, gripping the crumbling wood with both hands to hold it open.

"Hurry!" he cried.

Jo darted beneath his outstretched arms, followed by Lizzie. Vincent and Henry were drawing closer—but a deep snarl and a rattle of bone betrayed the horror of the revenants on their heels. Thorpe's eyes widened, and his muscles strained against Xabat's power.

Ten feet away. Five feet.

"Go!" Vincent shoved Henry in front of him. Henry stumbled but slipped through.

A hand grasped Vincent's coat.

He hurled all of his weight forward. A hideous stench rose around him, and Henry shouted his name.

He was through.

Thorpe leapt from the doorway, and the wood slammed shut behind him, sheering off the arm clutching Vincent's coat. The arm instantly went limp and fell loose, nothing more than a bundle of bone and dried tendon, its palm scabbed over with a fine dusting of tiny crystals.

"Vincent!" Henry started to catch Vincent to him, but Thorpe let out a warning cry.

"The door! She's opening it!"

Thorpe clung to the handle, using all his weight to hold it closed. Lizzie joined him, along with Jo and Vincent. "Henry, use your picks and lock it!"

Henry swore, but a moment later hit the ground at Vincent's feet. His shoulder pressed into Vincent's thigh as he worked, muttering furiously all the while. A heavy blow jostled the door, and the pick slipped out. "Hold it!"

"We're trying!" Jo exclaimed. She'd braced her shoulders against the door and her feet on the floor. "Hurry, Henry!"

"I'm going as quickly as I can," he snapped back. "Just...about... there..."

There came a loud click as the door locked.

They all let go with a sigh. Lizzie turned to Thorpe, who swept her into his embrace. "Are you all right, darling?" he asked her.

The door shuddered beneath repeated blows. Vincent hauled Henry to his feet, then glanced around to make certain they were all accounted for. Jo seemed shaken but unharmed. As for Miss Blake and Wellington, locked in with Xabat and the revenants, Vincent rather thought they deserved whatever befell them. "We need to get out of here, as quickly as possible. The door isn't going to hold forever."

Henry nodded. "Jo, are you all right?"

"I'm fine." She cast him a worried look. "Henry, your dad...the message we found in the classroom, the first day. I think it was from him."

Henry's lips tightened. "That makes sense. Is he still here, Vincent?"

Vincent took the pin from the pocket he'd shoved it into. "Yes. We'll give him peace, as soon as we get out."

"Which we need to do now, before they break through," Lizzie said, striding for the staircase.

"But what about Xabat?" Jo cast a fearful look in the direction of the cavern. "We can't just leave...what *is* it, even?"

"Hunger." Vincent shuddered. "It's not like anything I've ever seen before. Even the most evil ghosts have something human left within them. Xabat is nothing but hunger and hate. It fed on me. Made me feel as though I deserved to die, and all the while my despair just made it stronger."

Lizzie shook her head. "That doesn't sound like an ordinary ghost."

"The Astral Key might open doors to places other than the afterlife human souls pass to," Henry said. "Perhaps it's some other order of being."

"A demonic power, if so," Thorpe said. "But what does it want?"

"To feed." Vincent looked at the door, as though he could see the demon beyond. "You heard what it said. It wanted to put another of its kind in my flesh."

Henry paled. "Wellington's scheme to sell the Grand Harmonium to rich men...it wouldn't be their ghosts reborn in younger bodies, but creatures like Xabat."

"Which would then be able to use their power and wealth to spread more despair and chaos." Thorpe swallowed visibly. "Make the world into a feast of pain and anger."

Vincent nodded. "I'm afraid so."

"We have to stop it," Henry said.

"We don't have any weapons." Thorpe raked his hand back through his thick hair. "I hate to suggest running, but the revenants will surely tear us apart. Our only choice is to get out so we can warn others, before returning better equipped."

They followed Lizzie to the stairs. The iron spiral creaked alarmingly beneath their weight.

From the back of the line, Vincent heard Lizzie let out an oath. "Charles? I need your strong arm. It would seem the trap door has closed above us."

Vincent's pulse had started to steady, but her words brought it thundering back. "Closed?"

"There was no lock on it," Henry said. "And the mechanism on this side wasn't hidden. It should simply open."

"And yet, it isn't," Lizzie replied tersely.

Thorpe shoved against it, but the trap door failed to yield. Henry joined him, but after several moments of grunting and cursing, gave up. "Xabat must be playing the same trick as with the door back there. Holding it shut."

Silence fell over them. From the other side of the darkened basement, the sound of bodies hitting and clawing at the wooden door echoed.

"We're trapped," Vincent said. "And the door won't hold forever."

# CHAPTER 18

THEY DESCENDED THE uncertain stair and stood in silence. Henry put a hand to Jo's shoulder; she flinched with every thump of reanimated corpse against the door.

All these years, while he'd mourned his father, Henry's only consolation had been he was at peace. Even after Wellington, as Woodsend, had tainted Henry's memories, interrupted his grief, turned the aftermath of his father's death into something terrible.

Except there had been no peace. Wellington had taken everything as a twisted act of revenge, and stolen the final memento Henry had of his father. That was bad enough, but what Wellington had done…

This whole time, his father had been Wellington's slave. There had been no peace.

Wellington had enriched himself, pretending to be a medium, using the talisman to force Henry's father to interact with other spirits on his behalf, claiming the revelations for his own.

Fear warred with grief and pride. His father had been subjected to Wellington's evil whims, denied the rest he deserved. And yet, he'd done everything he could to protect Henry and Jo.

No doubt they'd be joining him on the other side sooner rather than later. There came a crack of wood; it wouldn't be long before the undead broke through.

"I'm sorry to have brought you here, Jo," he said. "I never imagined it would end like this."

"The fault is mine." Vincent moved to stand on Henry's other side. "If I'd just been able to let Dunne go…"

"And I should never have gone into business with that blackguard, Wellington," Thorpe said. "If only I'd known what a treacherous worm he was…well, we might still be in this position, actually."

Lizzie made a sound of exasperation. "Honestly, you men give up so easily." She took out her notebook and pencil, and seated herself in a rustle of skirts. "Vincent, bring me the stick pin, please. Jo, direct your lantern over here. A shame we left the head lamps in the cavern."

"The shirts wouldn't fit over the rucksack batteries," Jo said ruefully. "And the Harmonium would probably have just drained them anyway."

Vincent handed Lizzie the pin. She held it loosely in her right hand for a moment, eyes closed. "Spirit of Alfred Strauss, I call upon you. Help us, if you can."

Her left hand moved in lazy circles, the tip of the pencil drawing nothing but a loose doodle. Then, suddenly, it firmed.

*henry jo I'm sorry tried to warn you*

Henry's heart beat faster. Memories tried to crowd forward, of Wellington's false séances, pretending to speak for Father. None of that had been real. But this was.

Father was here. With him. Loving him, even beyond the grave.

"It's all right, Father," Henry said. His throat tried to constrict around the words, so he cleared it. "Is there any help you can offer?"

*the enemy of my enemy is my friend*

Vincent frowned slightly. "I don't understand. I mean, I understand the phrase, but I don't see how it's applicable."

*use the skull*

Perhaps Henry had misunderstood. Or Father had. "The skull? Arabella's skull?"

"Use it for what?" Thorpe asked bewildered.

*she is xabat's enemy tried to tell you tried to warn you both at once she was too strong for me*

Vincent grabbed Henry's hand. "The spirit writing Lizzie did before. That's why it didn't make any sense. Arabella and Alfred were trying to communicate at the same time, and their messages were intermingled."

Lizzie hastily flipped back in her notebook. "I copied it from the slate, just in case." She began to underline certain words, hesitated, then underlined others. "Here."

*not her he's lying to you it be wasn't careful her son release me something else came if you can back instead have but save to your stop self it falling pain first darkness cold have to stop I'm sorry it found him I love stopped you him now I will stop YOU.*

"He's lying to you," Henry read aloud. "Careful, son. Release me if you can, but save yourself first. I'm sorry. I love you."

He swallowed thickly against emotion. Vincent squeezed his hand, and read, "Not her. It wasn't her. Something else came back instead. Have to stop it. Falling. Pain. Darkness. Cold. Have to stop it. Found him. Stopped him. Now I will stop you."

Henry's stomach went queasy. "Arabella knew something had taken Mrs. Marsden's place. She had to act quickly, so she stabbed it—and inadvertently killed nearly everyone else at the same time. Her own brother attacked her, and she fell into the well. As she died, she must have clung to the thought the Grand Harmonium couldn't be used again."

"So when Dunne tried to rebuild it, she killed him, too." Vincent's voice was flat. "She knew it needed two strong mediums for the focus, so when we came here, she fixed on killing me."

"Let's not forget, she likely murdered my father to keep him from using the Astral Key." Thorpe shook his head. "We can't ally ourselves with such a creature."

There came another loud crack, followed by splintering wood. Jo swung the lantern around, revealing bodies squirming through the gap in the broken door. Lizzie set aside her notebook and rose to her feet. "We don't have a choice." She held the stick pin out to Henry. "This belongs to you."

Henry took it, grateful his fingers didn't shake. "Thank you." He tucked it carefully into his vest pocket.

"Vincent?" Lizzie prompted.

Vincent untied the sack with the skull. As the door crumbled and the dead stumbled into the basement, he pulled it free of its salty prison.

"I call upon the spirit of Arabella," he said in a commanding tone, lifting it high. "Xabat has returned! We want to destroy it, and destroy the Grand Harmonium, but we can't do so without your help!"

"Not to interrupt, but how exactly are we going to destroy Xabat?" Thorpe asked, looking from face to face.

Jo met Henry's gaze. "Reverse the flow of energy?"

"You mean instead of pulling from the other side, we push Xabat back into it? Yes. It could work."

"If we use the batteries in place of a circle—"

"Brilliant, Jo!" His heart leapt—then fell again. "But we have to be able to get to the Harmonium."

"Let us worry about that," Vincent said. "Arabella! Are you with us or against us?"

The temperature in the basement plunged, and frost raced across the floor around them. Between one breath and the next, she appeared before them, casting a sickly green light across their faces. Her hair hung limp around her face, and water dripped from her soaking dress. Crystals studded her body at intervals, and filled the sockets of her eyes.

"Help us!" Vincent said again, his voice like a whip crack.

Her lips peeled back, exposing teeth like crystalline needles. Then she whirled away and flew at the stumbling dead.

The dead were hurled back through the air, propelled by Arabella's immense strength. Dry bones snapped as they struck the floor and walls of the cavern. Arabella drifted out after them, her dress and hair moving as if caught in a current. She tasted of water and slime, of rot and blood, and it was all Vincent could do not to gag.

"She's cleared us a space," he said. "Lizzie, come with me. Henry and Jo, do whatever it is you mean to with the Harmonium."

Henry caught his hand. "Vincent...be careful."

The light of their lanterns reflected from Henry's spectacles. The corners of his mouth were tight with determination, but fear had stripped away what little color he had to start with.

"We'll buy you time," Vincent said, and squeezed Henry's fingers hard. "But be as quick as you can."

He pulled free and ran after Arabella. Lizzie followed him—as did Thorpe, the gun in one hand and a lantern in the other. Vincent didn't waste his breath pointing out the gun hadn't done anything to deter the risen dead earlier.

"The cavern enhances psychical ability," Lizzie panted. "I know they're clothed in flesh, but we might still be able to banish the risen spirits."

The cavern strengthened the spirits as well...but perhaps she was right. It wasn't as though Vincent had any other ideas.

"Together, then," he said.

They fell in side-by-side, as they had so often during their apprenticeship. Dunne had taught them to work together—no doubt so they could serve as foci for the Grand Harmonium. He pushed the thought aside. Dunne's motives no longer mattered. "The children may be the easiest," Lizzie said. "They never tried to attack us before. I think they were trapped here by Xabat, rather than their own obsession."

A revenant dressed in the sober clothes of a teacher lurched in Arabella's direction. A cluster of crystals speared from its mouth, nearly unhinging its jaw. Nevertheless, an eerie groan emanated from within.

Arabella snarled and struck. The revenant's hands passed through her—but she wrenched the crystal cluster out of its mouth. The jaw came free as well, and the revenant stumbled. Was it Vincent's imagination, or did it seem weaker?

He tore his attention away from Arabella and focused on the nearest of the child revenants. It had regained its footing and moved toward them with startling speed, given one leg now dragged behind it.

"Spirit," Lizzie said, and Vincent joined his voice with hers. "Your time here in this world is at an end. Go to your rest, and trouble this place no more."

The revenant's pace slowed, but it still continued toward them.

Vincent drew a deep breath, centering himself. He allowed all of the distractions to fall away: his worry Henry might not find a way to banish Xabat, his fear they might all die here in this cavern, torn apart by the corrupted dead. There was only himself, and Lizzie, and the revenant before him.

He remembered the laughter of the child ghost. How it had slammed doors as a prank. To condemn its spirit to this form, bound in mummified flesh, sharp crystals bursting out between its ribs, was cruel beyond measure.

They would help it. Free it. Fulfill their obligation to the dead and the living alike.

Vincent raised his hand, and out of the corner of his eye saw Lizzie do the same. "Spirit! Your time here in this world is at an end! Go to your rest, and trouble this place no more!"

H e *felt* it. Like sunlight against closed eyelids, or the release of a breath long held. Like a bubble of joy, rising to the top of a dark gray sea.

The revenant sank to its knees, slowly collapsed and lay still.

Vincent shifted his awareness, looking for the next revenant. Arabella had ripped Everett's remains to shreds, peeling away crystals until only inanimate leather and bone remained. Now she fought with the nurse, while Thorpe led the shambling body that must have belonged to Mr. Marsden in a wide circle, drawing him away.

Lizzie grabbed Vincent's hand, her focus already on the next child revenant. Vincent joined her, and moments later it fell. The third was already almost upon them. They would have to act quickly.

Lizzie's hand was ripped from his. She fell with a grunt, blood staining her pale hair. Startled from his trance, Vincent turned, just in time to duck as Miss Blake swung a broken length of crystal as long as her forearm at his head.

"You." Fury burned in her eyes, and she took another swipe, forcing him back. "I should never have listened to Wellington and suggested Thorpe look in Baltimore. You're all far more trouble than you could ever be worth."

Vincent tried to rush her, but the child revenant seized him from behind, pinning his arms to his sides. The sack containing Arabella's skull tore free and bounced away.

"Next time, we'll be more careful." Miss Blake lifted the crystal high, in preparation of staving in Lizzie's head. "For now, it's time to wipe the slate clean."

Henry raced across the cavern, Jo on his heels. Shouts and unearthly cries rang from the swarm of undead, but Henry didn't dare glance in that direction. If something happened to Vincent...

He thrust the thought aside. He had to concentrate, if they were to get out of the cavern alive.

"Jo, set up the batteries," he ordered. "I'll work on the Grand Harmonium itself."

Jo began to pull the batteries free of the rucksacks, scattering salt everywhere. Henry dropped his tool bag and snatched out wire, cutters, and a screwdriver. The Astral Key in its cradle seemed to mock him. Whatever properties it obeyed were still unknown to science, let alone to Henry. Half of what he was about to do would be guesswork.

But it was the only chance they had. Henry steeled himself, grabbed up the cutters, and clipped away one of the wires leading to the Astral Key's cradle.

Sweat slicked Henry's brow as he worked. Jo finished with the batteries and joined him. Together they rewired the connections between the Astral Key and the rest of the Grand Harmonium.

If only there were some way of knowing whether it would even function. To test it beforehand. But there wasn't.

If they failed, it would be the end of all of them. Xabat would never let them go.

"We'll only have one chance at this," he said to Jo. "Be quick as you can, but make certain the connections are correct. If—"

Rough hands seized Henry, wrenching him backward. He slammed into the ground, head barely missing the batteries. The pin went flying from his pocket, bouncing away across the floor. Stars spangled his vision at the impact with the stone, and for a moment he thought the shadowy figure standing above him belonged to one of the undead.

"What have you done?" Wellington snarled, a mad look in his eyes. Before Henry could roll away, Wellington dropped down to straddle him, weight pinning his hips in place.

"Stop!" Jo shouted. She rushed at Wellington, but he backhanded her, sending her to the floor.

Henry let out an inarticulate cry and flung a fist of his own. He was too slow, still dazed from the blow to his head. Wellington caught his wrist in one hand, and closed the other around Henry's throat.

"You would have been rich beyond your wildest dreams," Wellington snarled. Henry clawed madly at the hand compressing his windpipe, but Wellington only tightened his grip. "I would have been more than generous. But you refused. So I'll just have to make use of you another way." A maniacal grin spread over his features. "Don't worry, Henry. You'll soon be rejoined with your father…as my ghostly slave."

# CHAPTER 19

**"LIZZIE!" VINCENT SHOUTED.** He tried to lunge at Miss Blake, but the child revenant clung tenaciously to him.

"Vincent! Duck!" Thorpe called.

Vincent hurled himself violently to the side, dragging the revenant down with him. There came the crack of the pistol. Red blood splashed across the blue floor...and Miss Blake crumpled lifelessly.

Lizzie lowered her arm and looked up. Thorpe stood posed dramatically atop a rough outcropping of low crystals just off the smoothed floor. As Mr. Marsden's revenant tried to clamber over the uneven outcrop to reach him, Thorpe turned and flung his lantern.

Flame and oil splashed over the revenant, igniting cloth and leathery skin. It spun and flailed, arms thrashing in the air, until it collapsed into a twitching heap.

"Charles," Lizzie breathed.

"A bit of help, please!" Vincent shouted, as the revenant's teeth worried at his coat.

"Oh! Yes." Lizzie stood up, swayed, then regained her balance. Blood streaked the side of her face, but the injury didn't seem to be serious. "Spirit! Your time here in this world is at an end! Go to your rest, and trouble this place no more."

The revenant's limbs went slack. Vincent pulled free and rolled to his feet. Nearby, Arabella hurled aside the last remains of the nurse's revenant. Thorpe ran to them and caught Lizzie up in his arms.

"I love you, Elizabeth," he said, gazing down into her eyes.

She touched his face tenderly. "I love you too, Charles."

A growl of utter fury echoed through the cavern.

Xabat stalked toward them, the flickering flames revealing an expression of twisted hate on its face. Its black hair trailed a cloud of darkness behind it, and red light glowed in the depths of its eyes.

The first time it had been brought into Mrs. Marsden's body, it hadn't had time to gather its strength. Arabella had been able to strike it down with a simple knife.

But this time it had fed, glutting itself on fear and pain. Vincent had the horrible sensation it wouldn't be nearly so easy to get rid of now.

"Pathetic creatures," Xabat snarled. "How dare you take my followers from me? Hollow, broken things, caught up in your own petty desires. You are nothing compared to me."

Arabella turned to face the thing that had taken her mother's flesh. Her lips pulled back from teeth like blue needles, and she let out a growl of her own. She rushed forward, one arm drawing back, her nails sprouting into crystalline claws.

At the same moment, Xabat dove forward and snatched something up off the floor.

Arabella's skull.

Oh hell.

Arabella's spectral claws laid open Xabat's cheek to the bone. It didn't even seem to notice, drawing itself up with a horrible grin that gaped open the flesh and revealed teeth beyond. Blood poured down the side of its face.

It lifted the skull high—then slammed it down with stunning force against the rock. The skull shattered into pieces.

Arabella instantly became less solid. Without the skull, her hold on the world began to slip.

Only rage held her here now.

With the last of her strength, she hurled Xabat into the cavern wall. There came the snap of bone, and Xabat crumpled to the floor.

For a long moment, Vincent allowed himself to hope the blow had been a mortal one. But as a fading Arabella closed in, Xabat lifted its head at an impossible angle.

"Be gone," Xabat said, and the words echoed and echoed around the cave. The crystals seemed to glow in response.

Arabella's mouth opened as if in a scream of frustration. But no

sound came out. Her form became insubstantial: smoke, a wisp of fog...
and then nothing.

Xabat sat up. Blood stained its white shift, but it seemed unaffected
by its wounds. It gave Vincent a nasty grin through reddened teeth.

"You're next," it said.

Darkness spangled Henry's vision, and his lungs burned. The light
was dying. Or perhaps it remained the same, and it was Henry who
faded. If he died, would he be trapped here, as the other ghosts of the
orphanage had been, to be used as Xabat's plaything? Or would Xabat
allow Wellington to make good on his threat?

Another figure appeared over Wellington's shoulder. This one
wasn't a shadow, but stood out in extraordinary clarity, as if lit from
within. Despite the passage of years, Henry recognized the round face,
kindly eyes, and thick mustache as if he'd seen them yesterday.

Glowing hands seized Wellington. Wellington let out a startled
shriek, and the fingers gripping Henry's throat let go. His weight
vanished from Henry's stomach, and Henry rolled onto his side, gasping
and choking as sweet air rushed into his lungs.

Alfred Strauss stood before Wellington like an avenging angel,
burning with pure light. Wellington scrambled back, then staggered to his
feet.

"No!" he said. "You're mine to command. You have to obey me!"

"Not anymore," Jo said with grim satisfaction, and held up the stick
pin.

Wellington's eyes widened, and he began to back rapidly away.
"Don't—stay back—please—"

Alfred seized him by the lapels with unearthly strength. Wellington's
feet dangled above the floor. Blazing eyes stared into his.

"You'll never hurt my son again," Alfred growled, and heaved
Wellington into the air.

Wellington slammed into the cave wall, directly on top of one of the
great clusters of crystals. Blue points speared through his chest, belly, and
leg. His impaled body gave a single, convulsive jerk, before going slack.

Jo helped Henry to his feet. Alfred turned to them. His form seemed
already to be less substantial.

"I love you both," he said, but his voice was little more than a
whisper, fading fast.

Henry held out a hand. For a moment, he felt as though he were a
child again, standing by the graveside while his father was lowered into

the ground. "Don't go," he said in a small voice. "Please, Papa."

There was just enough left of Alfred to see his smile. "You have everything you need. Trust in your heart."

He was gone.

Tears burned Henry's cheeks. His father was finally at peace, and yet Henry couldn't help but feel as though he'd lost him all over again.

"Henry?" Jo said softly.

Henry swallowed. His whole body felt stiff, but he forced himself to turn to her. "Yes?"

Jo stood staring down at the batteries, an expression of despair on her face. "The batteries. Uncle Alfred drained them to get enough energy to save you." She looked up and met Henry's gaze. "We can't use them to operate the Grand Harmonium."

Xabat climbed to its feet, an arm dangling limp at its side. Blood coated one side of its face and matted its hair, but it bared its teeth in a ferocious grin. "Now that annoyance is out of the way, it's time to put an end to this little game."

Hopefully Henry had enough time to alter the Grand Harmonium, because they'd run out of options otherwise. "Fall back!" Vincent shouted.

They fled across the cavern, making for the Grand Harmonium. Wellington's corpse dangled horribly from crystal spikes, blood dripping on the ground. Henry and Jo were still on their feet, though both appeared rather the worse for wear.

Of Alfred Strauss, no trace remained.

"Dear lord, are you all right?" Thorpe exclaimed, staring up at Wellington's impaled body.

The left lens of Henry's spectacles was cracked, and bruises bloomed on his throat, but he nodded. "Father saved me from Wellington. But he had to drain the batteries to do it."

Vincent looked back the way they had come. Arabella had managed to injure Xabat's body, but it still made its way slowly toward them, one leg dragging behind. A horrible grin bloomed on its face as it relished their fear.

"We have no choice but to use the Harmonium," Lizzie said. She put a hand to Vincent's arm. "Every moment we dawdle is another moment Xabat regains its strength."

"At least we still have the shirts on," Henry said. He stepped into position and held out his hand.

They were all afraid, and weak, and Vincent honestly didn't know how much energy remained for them to give. Between the earlier turns at the Harmonium and the battle after, none of them had any reserves left. Not to mention they'd had five bodies to power the Harmonium before. Now they were down to three.

Arabella was gone, as was Alfred Strauss, and no other help was coming. They had only themselves, bruised and battered and exhausted.

Henry lifted his chin and met Vincent's gaze. "This is going to work."

Vincent swallowed. "How can you be sure?"

"Because I believe in us." He held his hand out, and Vincent took it automatically. "All of us. Together. We have the one thing Xabat doesn't. That it can't by its very nature."

"What?"

"Love."

"That's all very well and good, but we're out of time!" Jo exclaimed, taking up her place at the Grand Harmonium.

Vincent gave Henry's hand one last squeeze and stepped up to the focus. Lizzie took her position opposite him, and they both laid their hands on the metal plate.

"Vincent and Elizabeth," Xabat called. It was closer now, and to Vincent's horror its injuries had begun to heal. Dark smoke billowed from every footstep, and its eyes glowed with red fire. "You are nothing. Your own families cast you aside. How can you hope to stand against me?"

"Don't listen to it," Vincent said. "This is our family. Here."

"I know," Lizzie said. "Open the way."

Vincent turned his back on the horror coming closer. "The way is open."

His palms tingled, but nothing happened. If Henry's adjustments had failed...

"You failed as an inventor, Henry." Xabat's voice seemed to surround them now. "Even the Psychical Society didn't want your feeble tricks. Without your partners, you'd be nothing."

"But with them, I am something," Henry said. "Concentrate, everyone! Concentrate on each other. On the bonds binding us together."

The Grand Harmonium spun to life. Energy flowed, just as it had before, into Vincent, through him, and into the Astral Key.

But this time, it was more than energy.

He could feel each of them, all the little souls attached to his in the circle. Lizzie, his sister in every way but body, who had stood by him for so many years, and would so as long as they lived. Jo, who would do anything Henry asked, because he'd earned her trust and her love. Who looked to Vincent like an uncle or an older brother, with all the caring in her fierce young heart. Thorpe's adoration for Lizzie, bright as only the spark of new love could be.

And Henry. Proud, stubborn, wonderful Henry, with his mind full of gears and wires. Henry, who had given Vincent something he hadn't even realized he'd been missing: a true partner in life. Someone who might quarrel with him, but would never turn away. Henry, whom he loved as much as it was possible to love anyone, and who loved him in return.

This was his family: messy and beautiful and a little bit strange. They were his, and he was theirs.

The circle was complete.

"Open the gate!" Lizzie cried, and Vincent added his voice to hers. "Open the gate; open the gate!"

Golden light flared from the Astral Key, first as a glow, then as a beam of pure radiance. It shot out past them like a spear, and struck Xabat in the chest.

Xabat let out a scream of fury and pain. Light spilled from its half-healed wounds, as though fire consumed it from within. "No! No, you cannot do this to me! You're not strong enough!"

"Not apart," Henry agreed breathlessly. "But together we're more than a match for the likes of you."

"Xabat!" Vincent shouted, and the taste of his own blood filled his throat. "Foul spirit, the gate is open!"

"We bid you go through!" Lizzie's long hair rose from her shoulders, energy crackling all around them. "Leave this place and trouble us no more!"

Xabat shrieked and hurled itself at Henry. For a terrible instant, Vincent thought Henry would try to escape, breaking the conduit and causing the same backlash that had killed so many all those years ago.

Henry shut his eyes and stood firm and steady as a rock.

Even as Xabat's hands reached toward him, they began to crumble into dust. The years caught up to Mrs. Marsden's body all at once, flesh falling off of bone, then bone fragmenting in turn. Its scream grew higher and higher—

The golden light pulsed bright. A cold, putrid wind howled over them, blowing Vincent's hair back from his face, snatching at his clothing. The Astral Key flashed once again, before the beam of light diminished into a steady glow.

Xabat was gone.

"Let the gate be closed," Vincent ordered, and Lizzie chimed in. "Let the gate be shut, and never opened again."

The glow died away. Silence fell over the cavern, broken only by the sound of their breathing and the distant drip of water.

Henry took his hand off the plate. Jo cried out and hugged him. Vincent wrapped his arms around them both, and, alternately laughing and crying, they sank to the floor in a messy knot.

"I can't believe we're alive," he managed to say eventually. He kissed Jo's hair, then Henry's.

"I can't believe our alterations worked," Henry said with a shaky laugh.

"You're both geniuses." Vincent hugged them again, more tightly, then raised his head. "Lizzie, are you all..."

Lizzie and Thorpe were in each other's arms, mouths sealed together in a passionate kiss. "Never mind," Vincent said.

All the aches he hadn't allowed himself to feel started making themselves known. He struggled to his feet, wincing as his bones protested, before helping Jo up. Henry leaned heavily against the Harmonium to stand. "The ride back to the mansion is going to be a long one."

Vincent groaned at the prospect.

"At least we're alive to make it," Thorpe said. He reluctantly let go of Lizzie and stepped to the Harmonium. He removed the Astral Key from its cradle—and hurled it to the floor. The black stone cracked, but he stamped on it several times more, until nothing remained but fragments.

"Just in case," he said with a wry twist of his lips. He offered his arm to Lizzie. "Shall we?"

"I don't ever want to see another cave in my life," she said.

They led the way out. Jo leaned against Henry's right side, so Vincent put an arm around his waist from the left. Taking the last lantern, they walked out together, leaving the cavern and the Grand Harmonium to darkness and silence once again.

# CHAPTER 20

"**I RECEIVED A** letter from Lizzie," Vincent called as he came down the stairs into the workshop.

Henry glanced up from the equipment he'd been carefully checking over. They had a séance scheduled for later, and he wanted to be certain everything was in working order.

Six months had passed since the fateful night beneath Angel Mountain. At times, Henry felt as though the experience, terrible as parts of it had been, had lifted a cloud from their lives. Vincent smiled and laughed more than he had since Henry had known him. He'd made his peace with Dunne, put away the guilt and uncertainty of the past, and turned his face fully to the future.

Charles Thorpe had moved to Baltimore and become a silent partner in the shop. With the infusion of cash, they were no longer struggling to stay afloat. Combined with a modest increase in advertisement, the shop was well on its way to turning a profit for all involved.

Thorpe's relationship with Lizzie had proceeded apace, and they'd left for Europe a month ago. Jo would soon be joining them to attend university. Henry would miss her terribly, and hoped she would return once she was through with her studies. But her life was her own, and he wouldn't begrudge her following her own path. Her future, whatever she decided upon, would be brilliant.

"How is France agreeing with Lizzie?" Henry asked.

"France is agreeing quite well with Mrs. Thorpe." Vincent beamed at the letter, as if he'd personally arranged the entire thing himself. "They were wed on the voyage over by a parson traveling on the ship."

"Wonderful news." Henry set aside his tools and went to Vincent's side. "Please, tender my congratulations to the newlyweds when you write back."

"I will. It seems they intend to tour at a leisurely pace until Jo joins them, returning to the States sometime next summer, once they have her settled in." Vincent passed the letter to Henry. "This will be of interest as well: the demolition of Angel's Shadow is complete, according to Thorpe's man of business."

"Good riddance," Henry said. He adjusted his spectacles and frowned. "Lizzie wants to open the cave as some sort of tourist attraction?"

"It is a unique feature of the landscape. Not to mention the unusual properties of the crystals. I imagine any number of mediums would love to purchase permits to hold séances there, once word spreads."

Henry lowered the letter. The memory of everything they'd gone through in the cave still haunted his nightmares. "Do you think it safe?"

"Yes." Vincent plucked the letter from his hands and set it aside. "You and Jo dismantled the Grand Harmonium quite thoroughly. The parts have been scattered, the plans burned. All spirits are put to rest. There's nothing to worry about. Though that probably won't stop you from doing so."

"Probably not," Henry agreed. He paused and took Vincent's hands in his. "I'm sorry you never had a chance to speak with Dunne again."

"He loved Lizzie and me...and yet he likely did terrible things in his quest to restore the Harmonium." Vincent lifted one shoulder in a half-shrug. "In the end, I suppose he was a man like any other. Good and bad combined."

"I suppose. Still, seeing my father again..." Henry trailed off, trying to think how to phrase it. "Of course, I wish Wellington had never used the stick pin against him so. I never wanted him to suffer."

"I'm certain he doesn't regret a moment of it," Vincent said. "It allowed him to be there to save your life, after all."

"It did. And you're right. Still..."

Vincent tugged him closer. "You feel guilty because a part of you is glad to have seen him one last time, despite the circumstances."

Henry laughed and leaned against him. Vincent slipped his arms around Henry's waist, pulling him close. With a contented sigh, Henry snuggled closer. "You know me well."

"I like to think so." Vincent dropped a kiss on Henry's hair. "Your reaction is a natural one. No need to feel guilt for it, my love."

Before meeting Vincent, Henry couldn't imagine spending his life with a man. Now, he couldn't imagine otherwise. They had both come so far since the cold winter day they'd met, when the future seemed to offer nothing but gray loneliness. "I wish I could give you what Charles was able to give Lizzie. I hope they have a life as happy as his parents did together."

"As do I." Vincent pondered. "I never considered such a thing for myself—and honestly, I don't think Lizzie did either, until Charles told her about his parents. But it doesn't mean I don't feel..." He paused, clearly searching for the right words.

"We are bound together just as surely?" Henry suggested softly. "Til death do us part."

Vincent cupped Henry's cheek in his palm. "Oh, Henry. You should know by now there is something that outlasts even death."

Henry remembered the warmth of his father's regard, before he finally faded away for the last time. Remembered too those last moments at the Harmonium, when he'd stood with his mismatched family and felt the ties that made them as one.

"Let me guess," he said with a smile. "Love."

Vincent grinned. "I knew you were a smart man," he said, and bent down for a kiss.

# SHARE YOUR EXPERIENCE

If you enjoyed this book, please consider leaving a review on the site where you purchased it, or on Goodreads.

Thank you for your support of independent authors!

# AUTHOR'S NOTE

The Panic of 1873 was a real event—in fact, it was sometimes referred to as the Great Depression, until the one in the 1930s came along. The Panic brought about the end of the railway building boom begun after the Civil War. Fifty-five railroad companies failed within a span of months, abruptly destroying thousands of livelihoods.

The Grand Harmonium was inspired by John Murray Spear's God Machine. Spear was one of many colorful characters involved in the American Spiritualist movement, who passionately advocated for labor reform, women's rights, and the abolition of slavery. In the 1850s, he claimed a group of spirits including Benjamin Franklin had ordered him to construct the "New Motive Power"—a mechanical Messiah that would usher in Utopia. Needless to say, the results were less than hoped for.

# ABOUT THE AUTHOR

Jordan L. Hawk is a trans author from North Carolina. Childhood tales of mountain ghosts and mysterious creatures gave him a life-long love of things that go bump in the night. When he isn't writing, he brews his own beer and tries to keep the cats from destroying the house. His best-selling Whyborne & Griffin series (beginning with *Widdershins*) can be found in print, ebook, and audiobook.

If you're interested in receiving Jordan's newsletter and being the first to know when new books are released, please sign up at his website jordanlhawk.com.

Made in United States
North Haven, CT
22 December 2021